THE NIGHT SHE DIED

Roger Ormerod

This Large Print edition is published by BBC Audiobooks Ltd, Bath, England and by Thorndike Press®, Waterville, Maine, USA.

Published in 2004 in the U.K. by arrangement with Juliet Burton Literary Agency.

Published in 2004 in the U.S. by arrangement with Juliet Burton Literary Agency.

U.K. Hardcover   ISBN 0–7540–7797–7 (Chivers Large Print)
U.K. Softcover   ISBN 0–7540–7798–5 (Camden Large Print)
U.S. Softcover   ISBN 0–7862–6306–7 (Nightingale)

The text of this Large Print edition is unabridged.
Other aspects of the book may vary from the original edition.

Set in 16 pt. New Times Roman.

Printed in Great Britain on acid-free paper.

British Library Cataloguing in Publication Data available

Library of Congress Control Number: 2003116430

CHAPTER ONE

That morning I had taken our two boxers for a walk along the lane that fronts the house. It was early November, and too cold to allow them their more usual plunge into the Severn. But in any event, for ages there had been no otters around for them to play with. I blame it on pollution, surely a criminal act. But what could I do about it? Nothing.

Wrapped in these thoughts, I plodded along. Ours is the only house along that lane, which eventually terminates at a derelict farmhouse, so that I had not anticipated strangers in the district. Friends would have phoned to warn us of their intention. But clearly, on our return, something had been registered by the dogs' squat noses or floppy ears, as they ran ahead, pausing from time to time to look back and bark, and check that I was still there.

The house is called The Beeches, from the row of splendid trees that runs past our drive and along the lane. I call it a drive, but in fact it is simply a large area of lightly gravelled earth. Nothing more than a parking patch, really. And now, as I turned into the gateless entrance, I saw that it was justifying its description, because a car was parked there, a Volkswagen Beetle. Black. And the visitor must have been inside the house, because there was nobody in the driver's seat. At the sight of it, my memory stirred.

I called Sheba and Jake to heel and fastened on their leads. You never know. They are not aggressive; rather, they are too friendly. But not everybody likes dogs, and their somewhat boisterous approach can be a little frightening to those who do not, and panic-stricken flaps of the arms are not likely to convey a friendly welcome. Indeed, this can be interpreted by the dogs as unprovoked assault. So . . . one lead in each hand and leaning back against their exuberance, I headed round the side to the kitchen door.

Mary was waiting there for us. Clearly, therefore, she had felt it necessary to intercept me, and lay on a little background information.

'They're in the sitting-room, Richard. I'll look after the dogs, if you want to go right in,' she said.

'It was a bit muddy, in places,' I warned her.

'We'll soon see to that.'

The dogs had their own towels, and accepted hazards such as cleaning as being all part of the fun. But Mary could control them. She spoke their language. I took off their leads, and they stood there, panting, awaiting the game of trying to chew the towels to shreds to help along with the rubbing.

'It's a woman, Richard.' There was a hint of

warning in Mary's voice. 'She says she knows you. Seemed a bit of a bossy type to me.'

'Name?' I asked. 'Did she tell you her name?'

'She asked for you as Mr Patton, but when I told her you were out with the dogs, and told her I'd fetch Amelia, she just said, "Yes. Do that." And looked down her nose at me. But she didn't tell me her name.'

Whoever she was, she had not endeared herself to Mary. It is very easy to assume that she is our housekeeper, or a servant of some kind, whereas Mary had legally inherited a specific portion of the house in Amelia's uncle's will. She is now part of our family, an important part. To anyone who might suggest otherwise, my wife can return a cool and brisk response. As, too, can I.

'She didn't say why she wanted to see me?' I asked cautiously, and Mary shook her head. Too many people, knowing that I am a retired police detective inspector, take it for granted that I'm available as a private enquiry agent, who, not being recorded in the Yellow Pages, is not 'official', so will make no charge for his assistance. Fortunately, from having cultivated a low profile, I am now only rarely approached.

But, on that morning, it seemed that I was about to be, and I could only hope that my assistance would be sought in something minor and not too physical. Advice, perhaps—

3

something like that. I can be very free with advice.

I kicked off my rubber boots and stepped into my house slippers, washed my hands under the kitchen tap, and used Sheba's towel (after a bit of a struggle) on which to dry them. Then I relit my pipe, which had been lying cold in my jacket pocket, and headed for the sitting-room.

Others might call it a drawing-room, or a lounge, but that room contained all the comfortable furniture, my collection of books on open shelves, the few pictures and ornaments Amelia and I have collected over the years, and the gas fire that pretends it's a coal fire. A pleasant, cosy room, it was, in which to sit. So . . . it's our sitting-room. And sitting in there at this time, my wife on the settee and our unexpected visitor in a winged armchair, were two women between whom the static electricity was crackling. The air was almost sufficiently charged to raise the hair on my neck.

Two faces turned to me, one eagerly smiling, the other attempting to convey a warning. Amelia had, clearly, been given a hint or two as to the reason for this visit.

'Here he is now,' said Amelia, a hint of relief in her voice.

'Yes, of course.' Our visitor smiled. 'I recognised him at once.' Then she rose to her feet in one smooth, athletic unwinding,

4

standing very nearly my own height, and presenting her right hand.

She had known me at a glance, but of course she had expected me. She had come here (and how she had discovered my address I couldn't guess) specifically to see me, and with a smile that went so far as to suggest that I was expected to be equally pleased by this approach. I took her hand because common courtesy demanded it, but my mind was scrambling for a recognition. A WPC I had known? No—she wasn't that. And still her hand gripped mine, almost as though she had at last reached a haven, a safe and solid platform on which to place her explanation, the who and the why of her presence there.

Smiling softly now, she said, 'Connie Freeman.'

The Christian name of Connie meant something to me, but I couldn't focus on the surname. Then, suddenly, it was associated with violence, with a storm . . . with a murder.

Then I remembered her, those mocking brown eyes prompting me, the tumble of black hair (now streaked with grey)—the challenge in her stance. She was perhaps a little heavier than I recalled, around the hips.

'Freeman?' I asked. 'You've reverted to your maiden name? You were—yes, that's it. Connie Martin.'

'Harry divorced me.'

I glanced at Amelia, then back again. 'Could

5

he do that?' I asked, my knowledge of civil law being scanty. 'After all, it was enforced separation.'

Connie had been in prison. Was that grounds for divorce? Separation by bars!

She smiled very thinly, glanced at Amelia, and back again. 'I agreed. It saved trouble, and it suited me. I was happy to see the back of him, as you can well imagine. I could have petitioned for divorce, myself. After all, I had the solid grounds of his adultery, Mr Patton. I had that much.'

'That was never proved, Connie,' I reminded her, using my persuasive voice, 'and you know that very well. There was never any solid proof. Just his name and office phone number in Sylvia Thomas's notebook. As it could have been quite innocently, when you come to think about it. After all, Harry's work was all advisory—as an accountant. He could well have been doing nothing more guilty than trying to find her another home.'

'And her number in his!' she burst out triumphantly. I had never thought of her as being very intelligent. 'My man got that information for me.'

'The same reason applies,' I pointed out.

'My man . . .' But she didn't pursue that. Her man! He had called himself a private investigation officer. It sounded good. But I had known, only too well—though I hadn't mentioned it at the time—that he had been dismissed from the force for accepting bribes. Poor Connie had not had much in the way of solid support. But now that was not relevant to Connie's obviously aggressive attitude.

'And you have to remember,' I reminded her, 'that the actual so-called adultery was never proved.' In court, her barrister had tried to build up into a solid background the amount of information he'd accumulated in regard to Harry's sexual activities, in the hope of proving extenuating circumstances, but it had not impressed the jury. It would, of course, have been relevant to any violence Connie might have inflicted on Harry, but was in no way a justification for the killing of his mistress—although it did indicate that Connie would have had a motive for attacking Sylvia.

At the present time, though, I was concerned only with the fact that Connie was now divorced. She was now Connie Freeman.

It was probably Connie's attitude that brought Amelia to her feet. 'Will somebody please tell me . . .' she asked, her tone so cold that the two dogs, entering abruptly with Mary, stopped still in the doorway, making soft whining noises. Amelia leaned over to pull an ear or two, to relax them, when they came close enough, then she tossed her head.

'. . . tell me what you two are talking about. I've got a right to know.' This was unusual from Amelia, who normally would prefer to remain in the background in circumstances

7

such as this. But she was reacting to the words 'mistress' and 'adultery'.

'Of course you have, my love,' I agreed, wondering myself where we were heading. 'The fact is that this visitor of ours, Connie Freeman, faced a court trial, and was found guilty of the murder of her husband's mistress. That was eight years—'

'Ten,' put in Connie Freeman. 'Nearly ten years ago, Sylvia Thomas died. Nine years I've been in prison for it.'

'Oh dear,' said Amelia, her tone indicating that, had I taken up with a mistress, she would probably have done the same thing. 'And they sent you to prison for that?'

'They did. Your husband's bumbling investigation did.'

'Richard!' Amelia appealed, gripping for my arm and shaking it. 'How could you?'

'Just doing my job, love,' I assured her. 'The evidence was overwhelming, and the court had all the facts and the details. In any event, the jury came up with a guilty verdict, and she was sent to prison.'

'How terrible!' Amelia cried, shocked, gripping my arm even more tightly, as though I had been solely responsible for this unfair decision by jury and judge. 'But somebody ought to *do* something. It's not right! Her husband's mistress! She deserved all she got.'

What she, the mistress, had got had been a head bashed in with a conveniently placed rolling-pin, one of those old ones with a wooden rod through it and a handle at each end. The handles had been covered with flour. Whether this was the reason that the forensic squad failed to develop any prints, or whether it was because the assailant had been wearing gloves, we had not been able to decide.

Remembering this, I grimaced at Amelia, who made a gesture of distaste, and asked, 'So why is this woman here, Richard?'

'Suppose we ask her that,' I said, and turned to face Connie Freeman again. 'Why *are* you here, Connie?'

She threw back her head, hair bobbing, registering righteous dignity. 'Because you're the one who knows all the facts. Oh . . . I'm sure you'll tell me you were working under orders of a superintendent or somebody like that—some big-bug, anyway—who knew nothing about it. Only what was put down on paper for him to read. "Ah!" he'd say to himself. "It's all too obvious. Connie Martin did this"—I was Martin then. "Better have her in and charge her." And it would be one more file to put away. One more for his record.'

Her voice had tailed off gradually, as though she had rehearsed this statement, over and over, until she had perfected it, every tone of righteous outrage and despair carefully honed to strike exactly the correct emotional impact, eventually to lure me into a position where I would find it impossible to reject what had to be an appeal to my conscience. She was relying on the assumption that I had a conscience, whereas police activities had always been unemotional, with no place for one's personal feelings.

I realised that I had to be wary, conceding as little as possible. The two women were now facing each other, sharing the opinion that men were hopeless when adultery entered into the situation.

'We're not getting anywhere,' I put in. 'And you really know very little about police activities, Connie. The super wouldn't make that decision. It would have to go to the legal experts, for them to decide whether we had a good, solid case. Or not. The Crown Prosecution Service, they call themselves, now. You can see—or at least I hope you can see—that I was a very small cog in all this. All I did was put in reports and statements, as and when required.'

Amelia was now sitting very upright on her seat, her eyes darting from face to face. 'Do you remember all this, Richard?' she asked.

'Yes. I remember it.' And the more we spoke it, the faster the memories were flooding back.

Connie perched herself on the very edge of her seat, both of the dogs having by now approached to consider this guest. I should have asked Mary to keep them away, as I wanted nothing distracting to intervene. But

Connie was clearly a dog person. She fussed each one until they both moaned with ecstasy. Amelia sat and watched, but said nothing. Neither she nor the dogs seemed perturbed. Indeed, Amelia was now smiling.

'It's what I missed so much,' Connie explained. 'In prison. Dogs. I've always had at least one dog, from the time I was a little girl. I had two cocker spaniels when they arrested me. My husband—you remember Harry . . .'

I nodded. I remembered Harry Martin very clearly. An accountant, he'd called himself.

'What about Harry?' I asked.

'He had them put down,' she said in a flat, cold voice.

'Oh . . .' Amelia whispered.

'So I've decided,' went on Connie, 'that when you've sorted it out for me, and I've got the time to spare, I'm going to have *him* put down. Harry. Put down. I can't get those two words out of my mind. Put down. Such a cold, blank statement. But I've found out all sorts of interesting information. I mean . . . you meet all sorts of women, inside. And I've got three names and addresses from three of my friends in there. Men friends of theirs, who would do a bit of putting down on my behalf . . . when I've got together enough money to pay for it. You'd be surprised how much they charge.'

'Now hold on, here!' I put in briskly, glancing at Amelia to see how she was taking this. Her eyes were bright, unblinking, two

11

fingers to her lips to intercept any indiscreet words that might be struggling to get free. Or even laughter.

'I missed the dogs,' Connie explained emptily. 'Just taking them for a walk. They'd got dogs there, you know, at the prison, lovely Alsatians. But only for show. Patrolling, they called it. I asked if I could take one of them for a run, but they wouldn't let me. Thought I might steal it, I suppose.'

'No,' I said, staring at my cold pipe, at anything that wasn't Connie's face. She was so solemnly calm about it, brought it out so naïvely, that I had to assume she was telling the truth. 'They wouldn't,' I added.

'Lovely Alsatians,' she repeated moodily. 'Do you mind if I smoke?'

'Go ahead,' I said, reaching into my pocket for my lighter.

Then Mary—and I hadn't realised she was still in the room—fetched the three-legged small round table from across in the far corner, placed it between Connie's chair and my own, and put one of our glass ashtrays on it. Connie turned her head, smiled up at Mary, and said, 'Thank you.' Then she began to root around in the floppy shoulder bag she had with her, and produced a gold cigarette case and gold lighter. I watched as she lit her cigarette.

'You didn't use that case and the lighter in prison?' I asked. 'Surely not?'

'Heavens, no! They'd have had them off me

in ten seconds.' She grimaced as she recalled her experience. 'But I've been home . . . *my* home, I still call it, in my mind, only it looks and feels all different. My son, Philip—did you ever meet him? Oh, of course you did, but he's twenty-six now, and he's got a live-in girlfriend there. In my home! You'd remember her. It's the same girl he was going around with at that time. Penny, her name is. Anyway, when I got home, there they were. And . . . d'you know . . . I felt I wasn't welcome in my own home. But I'll sort all that out. The bungalow is mine, you know. My father gave it to me. But of course, you know that. It's mine, and I can do what I like with it.'

Yes, I knew all about her bungalow, but I was trying to keep her on the same subject. 'Your son and the girl . . . what of them?'

She waved a hand; wiggled her fingers. 'The girl seems all right to me. Not a slouch, you know. Got a good head on her shoulders, and I'll say this about her, she's kept the place clean and tidy. And all I need is a room and a bed, to lay my head down. And—of course—your help, Richard. May I call you Richard?'

'You may.' But I wasn't so sure about my help.

I watched as she drew deeply on her cigarette, then she leaned over, and, with the tips of her thumb and first finger, she nipped off the red, glowing end, only a fraction of an inch from burning herself.

13

She looked up into my face, and laughed at my expression. 'I've always done that,' she told me.

'Don't you ever burn your fingers?'

She shook her head, pouting. 'Oh no. You just have to guess it right. Then, you see, you don't waste anything. And it was so useful, inside. If you tamp out a cigarette, it all crumples up, and you can't afford to waste anything like that, inside. Inside . . . inside . . . I can't get that word out of my mind. But . . . no waste if you pinch them out.'

I glanced at Amelia. She merely lifted her eyebrows at me. Clearly, she was completely baffled.

'And why have you come here?' I asked Connie.

'Surely that's obvious.'

'Not to me,' I assured her, though in fact I did have an idea, and I wasn't pleased with it. Definitely not.

She looked at Amelia, gave a little shrug at her lack of response, and concentrated once again on me.

'Because you're the one who collected all the facts,' she explained. 'The evidence, I suppose you'd call it. So you're the obvious one to put it all together again, and investigate it once more, to see where you went wrong.'

'Now hold on—'

She completely ignored my interruption. 'And then, when you've got it all sorted out,

14

with all the *new* evidence, we'll take it to my solicitor and we'll have another trial, only this time with the person who really killed that bitch my husband had tucked away. Sylvia Thomas. It wasn't me, so I suppose it has to be somebody else. With *that* person in the dock, this time. And I'll be able to claim damages, great loads of damages, for wrongful detention, and you can have some of it, for your trouble, though why you would deserve it I can't imagine, you being the one who got me put away.' She took a deep breath. 'But all the same, I'll give you a quarter of what damages they award me. Now . . . how does that sound to you? And this time it ought to be easier for you to get the right answer.'

She stopped, splayed her palms, and smiled ruefully at Amelia.

'Why easier?' I asked cautiously. Amelia moved uneasily on her seat.

'Because you can eliminate one suspect, to start with.'

'Who's that?'

'Well . . . me, of course. Oh . . . you *are* slow. Of *course* me.'

'There's no "of course" about it,' I told her. 'You probably picked up this idea inside. You'd be surrounded by women a darned sight more experienced than you, when it comes to twisting the evidence around and blurring the issue. Probably, they'd know all about that in their early teens —'

15

'You won't have to twist anything,' she assured me, blandly interrupting. 'You had your go at blurring the issue at the trial, and now I want it all laid out. Crystal clear. I want you to prove that I didn't do it. If the only way to do that is for you to produce the one who did, then that's what you've got to do.' She nodded emphatically. So there!

'Got to?' I asked, very quietly.

'You owe me that.'

'Hmm!' I said.

The truth was that it was to myself that I owed it, assuming that I had got it all wrong, the first time. I would need to reach very deeply into my memory, and attempt to discover a completely new scenario in which to place the death of her husband's mistress, Sylvia Thomas, and then eventually I would be in a position to shout out to all who might be interested: 'I was a clumsy, stupid oaf, who bungled it the first time.' It was not a pleasant prospect to have to contemplate.

The only thing I could think of which might persuade her that she was proposing an impossible task for me, was to remind her of a selection of the points of evidence against her. And first, I had to locate her at the scene of the murder of Sylvia Thomas. We both had to think back ten years.

'Your car was seen on that parking patch.' This was a try-on. Nobody had claimed that they had seen her car.

16

'No, it wasn't,' she said sharply. 'And anyway —think back to it. I'd bet anything you like that nobody could've even *seen* that parking patch from the houses. Don't you remember the weather, Mr Patton? Don't you? The visibility.'

I smiled. Yes, I remembered it. And she was quite correct. It had been a terrible day, and an even more terrible evening, once it became really dark. And Connie had claimed that, although her intention had been to visit Sylvia Thomas, to introduce herself as Harry's wife and to warn her off, the weather had prevented her from carrying it through. We didn't believe her. She had said she had driven off the road and on to that terrible parking area, when there was a proper lay-by only a couple of hundred yards away, which she could have used. And that she had tried to park her Beetle on the extensive earth patch used for parking, and had trouble with the muddy surface. She hadn't dared to stop, she had claimed. We didn't believe her. The visibility, I recalled, was perhaps four or five feet, with pelting rain, and not a light penetrating that rain curtain, anywhere. But she *could*, with determination, have parked only a hundred yards from Sylvia Thomas's house, rain and muddy conditions notwithstanding, if she had already driven there—although the appalling weather would have made it very difficult.

All this had been brought up at the trial,

and she had not been believed. There seemed no point in arguing about it now, so I tried another angle.

'There had been cigarettes smoked in Sylvia Thomas's kitchen. And your husband, Harry, didn't smoke cigarettes. Sylvia did, yes, but not Harry.'

'He does now.'

It was irrelevant. 'They were the brand you smoked, Benson and Hedges. That was the point I wished to make.'

She lifted her head. The smile she offered was one of complete confidence. But she had had a long while to think this through, and had prepared herself for anything I might query.

'So did she,' she claimed. 'His mistress—she smoked them, too.'

'And how do you know that?' I asked, very casually because it was a trick question. She had claimed that she had never come face to face with Sylvia Thomas, had only seen her across the saloon bar in sundry pubs. Perhaps she had seen Sylvia smoking there.

'Because,' she said, so demurely and so confidently, 'my precious husband pocketed a full pack of my cigarettes, on the evening when he said he was going to his office to finish checking an account—the liar. I phoned his office half an hour later, giving him time to get there, and got no reply. From either of them. He's got offices in Bridgnorth and Wolverhampton, you know. Damn it, Mr

Patton, it was the insult in it, the insult to my intelligence. He treated me as though I was stupid. As you'll no doubt remember,' she continued, after she had mastered a severely bubbling anger, '*he* smoked a pipe, the same as you. But did you pick up that point? You did not. No . . . let me say this.' She held up a palm. 'Once and for all. He had the utter gall to take my cigarettes for that mealy-mouthed bitch. Certainly not for himself, that's what I'm trying to get across to you.'

'All right. All right.' We were wandering far away from the point at issue, which was whether I was prepared to look into the case again, and it was beginning to seem that I was already trapped into conceding. And in fact there had been the remains of three Benson and Hedges cigarettes in an ashtray at Sylvia Thomas's home. I could see them now.

My memory is not at its best for words or numbers or facts; it is mainly visual. Sitting at my desk and reporting a motor vehicle accident, I could recall a clear picture of the scene. But the names and addresses of the people involved—no. For that I would have to resort to my notebook.

And now, my memory recording an image of that ashtray in Sylvia Thomas's kitchen, I knew I would have to go along with Connie's wishes, much as I might detest the idea.

'Very well,' I said to Connie, laying on a tone of reluctance. 'I'll have another look at it.'

'The whole case?' asked Connie eagerly, because she hadn't expected to be able to persuade me. I caught Amelia's eye, and registered her disapproval, then turned back to face Connie.

'You said you're back at the same house, with your son and his woman friend. Your own bungalow, if I remember it correctly.'

'Yes.' And now Connie was whispering, caught by the wonder that she had managed to persuade me, if only so far as to show interest.

'And your husband—Harry? Ex-husband, rather.'

'He's living with his latest woman. Jean Clarke. It's her flat, really. And oh—you've got to laugh. I went to visit them. I need to weigh up his attitude, which, if you must know, was a bit cool. And she—this Jean—she hid herself behind a chair. She's quite safe. I didn't kill Sylvia Thomas, so I'm not likely to start killing his new women. He keeps swapping around, you see.'

'Yes,' I said. 'Now you're out of prison, they'll *all* be nervous.'

And Connie laughed aloud. It was not a very good laugh, but it had probably had little exercise in the past few years.

'Well,' she said now, levering herself to her feet, 'I'll leave you in peace.' As though she had upset us. 'You wouldn't like to lend me one of your dogs? No? Pity. Never mind . . . I'll get one from a breeder I met inside. She's very lucky to have a daughter who's kept her kennels operating. How lovely for her. Such a lovely daughter! I'll find my way out. Don't trouble . . .'

But Mary was already troubling, holding the door open.

I got to my feet. You have to be polite. 'I'll be in touch.'

Then, Amelia seeming disinclined to remove herself from her chair, I went out with Connie, to see her off. To myself I had to admit it was a pleasure to watch her go, but I knew I hadn't seen the end of it. I could not blankly refuse to carry out her wishes. Not now. And in any event, if I *had* been wrong about Connie's guilt, then I wanted to be the first to know.

I watched as Connie drew on her driving gloves. The Beetle looked as though it would be draughty. I didn't wave as she started the engine and drove away, but simply turned and walked back into the house, finding that Amelia had come to watch and was pouting her disapproval on the doorstep.

'Well . . .' she said. 'Now you've gone and got yourself involved in another ridiculous and unpleasant investigation. And don't look like that, Richard. You're pleased, really. Admit it. Something for you to do. The last time, you said it *would* be the last. How could you, Richard? How *could* you?'

21

'Well . . .' I tried to smile. 'I've already come across one detail that I misinterpreted during the original investigation, my love. And *that* might not be the last detail to find.'

'What detail?' Amelia demanded cautiously.

'Well—you know my memory's mainly visual . . .'

'You're always saying that.'

'It is, though. And even now, after all this time, I can get a clear image of that ashtray on the corner table in the kitchen, where Sylvia Thomas—the mistress who was murdered— where she was found.'

'Yes, Richard . . . don't keep reminding me.'

'I can see it now. That ashtray, full of squashed-out cigarettes.'

'And? *Do* get to the point, Richard.'

'And, my love, they *were* all squashed out, and you saw what Connie did—and said she'd *always* done—when she wanted to put out a cigarette, even before she went to prison. She pinched it out—and in that ashtray there were no pinched-out cigarettes. Such a minor thing, but I missed it at that time. So . . . doesn't it sound, now, as though she could have been innocent, after all, and that she'd not even been there—as she claimed.'

'Richard!' she said, a little forcefully. 'You're always doing that . . . letting yourself be persuaded! Now . . . the clue of the squashed cigarettes! You *are* the limit. You're always twisting things around until you can see

22

what you want to see.'

'But it isn't just that,' I protested. 'You get a discrepancy like this—and she couldn't have thought it up herself and planned to use it— you've met her now. What d'you make of her? Naïve? That, certainly enough. Not too intelligent? That's surely established. But if she didn't kill Sylvia Thomas, then there's been a terrible miscarriage of justice, and based on my own evidence. How can I possibly refuse to go ahead with it?'

'By saying no.' But Amelia couldn't conceal the hint of a smile.

'I can't say no to myself, love. There's doubt—I'd never rest.'

'Richard!' She touched my arm, raised herself on to her toes, and kissed me on the end of my nose. 'You're a gullible fool, and I love you . . . and when do we start?'

CHAPTER TWO

We had, in fact, already started, as I had sent my mind tracking back into the past—and at once had come to a dead halt. My memory needed a boost or two. It needed, in fact, my notebook for the period involved. But you have to hand in your notebook on retirement or on transfer—or on blank dismissal. My category, hovering at that time, had been very close to ignominious dismissal, but even if I had managed to accomplish a decent and dignified retirement, the same fate would have been accorded to my notebook. It had been impounded, and now rested meekly in the police archives.

But—notebook or not—I could never forget the storm that night, and the flooding that had made our task so difficult. Such memories become locked in the mind. The river, at its peak, had been passing—no, rushing in a torrent is more like it—rushing past within a foot of the open rear doorway of the house . . .

'When do we start?' Amelia repeated. 'You're miles away, Richard.'

'Sorry, love, but my mind *was* miles away—around four miles the other side of the town bridge, to be exact. That was where it happened. But, and this is a distinct drawback, I've got no access to my notebook from that

24

time, because I had to hand it in. So I'll have to rely on my memory.'

'What's the difficulty, there?' she demanded. 'It'll all come flooding back.'

I couldn't stifle a short and rather bitter laugh. 'Flooding is the word. There'd been very heavy rain through the country, for a whole week, and the Severn was a roaring torrent. There was no access at all to the rear of the house.'

'Show me,' she said. 'Don't just stand there, talking about it. Show me.' Amelia was plainly becoming deeply involved in Connie's situation.

'Now?' I asked.

'Why not now? It's as good a time as any other.'

'Yes,' I agreed. 'Let's do that.'

And suddenly, with that decision made, I became restless, and eager to get going. So we explained to Mary what we intended to do, and I told her we couldn't take the dogs. But that was because of my sudden image of how the flooded riverside walk had been at that time, another November, ten years ago. It wouldn't be like that now. Yes, of course we could take them, I agreed, when Amelia pressed me for an explanation.

So, using Amelia's car, with Sheba and Jake on the rear seat, we set off. I told Mary to give us an hour or so, but I anticipated rather less than that. The run along to the town took barely five minutes, then across the bridge, and my objective was only four miles further up the river. Easy.

At least, it would have been easy, if I could have remembered exactly which turn-off to take. The road veered a good quarter of a mile from the river, so that from there my objective was not visible. I had to guess which left-hander to take. At the end of that side road, if I was correct, there had originally been a ford, a long time ago, when mobility involved horses. But more recently—fifty or sixty years ago—the ford had been replaced by a ferry, a flat, floating platform, wound over with a winch. More recently still, distances and detours becoming less important with the growth of motor traffic, the town bridge has performed the same purpose. But still, I hoped the parking patch for which I was aiming would be where my memory prompted me to go, and indeed, the parking sign was still there, much battered and undecipherable. But I recognised it; the same weary tilt.

I turned along that narrow access lane, the tarmac terribly pot-holed, remembering it now very clearly. We had had some difficulty with our police vehicles, I recalled.

Then, there it was, the slightly undulating and extensive patch of naked earth to our right. Even a remnant of the entrance sign was still guarding it—guarding something no longer used, I guessed. To our far left was the

26

meagre and pot-holed spur of tarmac, which was supposed to be the front access to the row of ten two-storey terraced houses. Sheds and two larger versions, clearly intended as garages, ran along the opposite side of this tatty driveway. These were new to me. Along there was what the residents would call their 'fronts'. Their rears faced the river.

It was the river walkway along their rears that I wanted to show to Amelia. From the far edge of the parking space a path led, becoming steadily more steep, until we were down on the riverside walkway. This ran, to our left, from a corner of the parking patch and along the run of the river.

This pathway would at one time have allowed you to walk, beside the river, all the way back to the town bridge, but it had been so little used, and quite neglected, that it now ran, in that direction, only a few yards past the end of the row of houses. In the opposite direction, neglected shrubbery and trees completely barred any access.

The short row of dwellings seemed to have lost its original purpose. At one time, at least one of the families would have operated the ferry. Now, the houses probably accommodated farmworkers, in the main, and maybe a few office or shop workers, employed in the town.

We stood on the path beside the river, and looked along the row of rear entrances. To our right there fell a steep, grassed bank, an average of four feet high, down to the water surface. Beneath our feet was the rough path, four feet wide, providing access to the rear of each of the houses. Why, I could not imagine. No tradesmen would venture along here, when the fronts were nearest. No hikers could fight their way through the packed greenery at each end, which ran down to the river, leaning towards the water and dipping stray and fractured branches into it. Yet, along this row of ten houses, raised on a bank about five feet high from the path, were steps up to each of the back doors, with wrought-iron handrails each side, these supported by iron railings. They could serve no practical purpose now, it seemed.

When we reached the end-but-one house, I stopped, and touched Amelia's arm. 'This is it, love.'

'It's what?' she asked.

'The house where Sylvia Thomas lived and died. Harry Martin's mistress. Her father had been a farmworker, but at that time she was living here alone. From the enquiries we made, we got the general impression that she wasn't liked. The neighbours turned their noses up at her, as her way of life was a little too blatant for them. You can imagine, with this set-up, that they would know all about her visitors. Oh yes, Connie's husband, Harry, wasn't the only one. And, we gathered, Sylvia Thomas wasn't at all secretive about her clientele. She

28

couldn't have cared less about her neighbours' opinions.'

'So . . .' said Amelia, urging me on, and grimacing her distaste.

The dogs were straining at their leads, anxious to explore a brand-new territory. I had a lead in each hand. 'Quiet, now,' I said to them, and they each sat down, but panting eagerly.

'It's not valid, you know,' said Amelia, as I hadn't responded. Her mind is apt to jump around.

'What's not valid?' I asked.

'That supposition from the squashed or non-squashed cigarette stubs in the ashtray. It's negative. No nipped-out remains, indeed! Connie Freeman, if she'd come here, visiting her husband's mistress, wouldn't have smoked. Think of it. If she'd come here in order to give her a piece of her mind—as she'd no doubt have thought of it—she'd hardly have been in a mood for smoking. She wouldn't have come here for a cosy chat and a quiet cigarette. Oh no. It would've been bitter words and angry threats. Can you imagine anything different, Richard? "Have one of mine!" Oh, I think not.'

'All right,' I said. 'All right. Angry words, then. Threats. And, Amelia love, a handy weapon on the kitchen table, as Sylvia Thomas had been rolling pastry, at the time. There was the rolling-pin, lying on the floor beside the table. Covered in flour, of course. What hadn't been washed away. It was the murder weapon—blood on it—and our forensic people couldn't lift any fingerprints from it, because of all the flour. And *anyway*—and this was something that we didn't pick up at the time—you saw what she did, leaving our place: Connie pulled on her driving gloves. So, whatever she did in this house, if she was wearing her gloves that evening, there wouldn't have been any fingerprints on the rolling-pin. Or rather, needn't have been, though it seems that she *must* have taken off her gloves, sometime while she was here.'

'Why d'you say that?' She was frowning as she considered it.

'Because, love, we found her prints elsewhere. Thumbprint, anyway. A single thumbprint.'

'Hmm!' she said. 'And nobody heard anything? Not one of her neighbours? There'd have been raised voices, you know. They wouldn't have discussed Harry Martin in controlled and polite tones.'

'No. I suppose not.' I smiled at her, because there was more to tell. 'There was the noise from the river,' I explained.

'Noise? It doesn't seem noisy to me.' She turned and looked round at the placid Severn.

'Ah yes—but I haven't told you about the weather,' I admitted.

She sighed. 'It's like trying to get blood out

of a stone. Do tell me, Richard, and stop going all round it.'

I had every intention of telling her, but there was a lot to be told, and I needed to organise my memory.

'Right then,' I said. 'It was November, as it is now. But whereas we're getting normal November weather today, what we had then was far from normal. It rained, poured with rain, and had been doing so for over a week, and there was no sign of an optimistic weather forecast.'

'I remember that,' Amelia said.

'Then you'll probably remember the flooding. The river was high. The path we're standing on now wasn't even visible, and the river was all brown with picked-up earth. And you'll have noticed, love, that we're on the outside of a curve. The water flung itself past here, and the roaring noise it made meant that we had to shout to each other. Even when we got inside the house, by way of the front door, we were still having to shout against the noise. On this bend, the water piled up, all sorts of debris tossing around in it. And this path was four or five feet under water.'

'You're talking about how it was looking from inside?' she asked, glancing round her, and trying to visualise it.

'Yes. We had that rear door open. It *was* open, when we got here. All the other houses—and, oh dear, the panic they were

31

in—*they* had their rear doors firmly locked and bolted, and were gathering stuff together. Old sheets and pillows, and that sort of thing, to try to block off the bottoms of their rear doors. At that time, the water swinging round the bend was making so much noise that we were having to shout —'

'You've said that, Richard. You and your team?'

'Yes. My team. Myself and the sergeant, at that time.'

'So why didn't you close the door?'

'Because we had to leave it as we found it, love. For the photographer and the rest of the forensic experts. All we could do—Sergeant Carter and myself—was to look around, and touch nothing. Just look.'

Amelia was silent, which gave me time to re-create in my mind the scene as it had revealed itself. The body of Sylvia Thomas had been lying face down, her head twisted, cheek to the water-soaked floor, and only two or three feet from the open rear doorway, the door restrained in an open position by one of her shoulders. Her arms were stretched out, as though her fingertips were fighting for a hold on the floor. The tumbling and thunderous water was right up to the last step short of the door frame, and the spray which had soaked the floor was beading her hair.

When I had told Amelia all these details, as clearly as I could recall, she asked, 'Where was the rolling-pin you mentioned?'

'On the floor,' I told her. 'Beside the table. In the middle of the room.'

'Ah! So she'd got as far as rolling it out.'

'Yes.' I had to agree, though I hadn't expected that Amelia would become so involved with it. Just casual interest, that was what I had imagined. Not the petty details.

'Sylvia Thomas had got as far as rolling out her pastry,' I went on, trying to keep the details as correct as possible. 'Connie Freeman must have gone first to the front door. One glance at the river—one ear cocked for the sound of it—would have been enough to tell her that there could be no access along the walkway. Along this path we're standing on. No doubt, when the weather was normal, the gentlemen customers would have used this walkway to the rear door.'

'You're assuming it *was* Connie.' Amelia gripped my arm and shook it. 'You're still assuming that.'

'The evidence,' I assured her, 'was overwhelming.'

'Hmph!' For some reason, Amelia seemed to have taken to Connie. Perhaps this was because Connie liked dogs. To Amelia, that reasoning would have been quite logical. 'So tell me,' she added.

This I did, but that was about a quarter of an hour later, by which time I had driven back to Bridgnorth, rehearsing it in my mind, recalling it. There, we had parked on the extensive grass-surfaced parking space, just short of the bridge, and were seated on one of the benches, watching the river placidly streaming past. We could just see the near-vertical railway that carried people up from Low Town to High Town. And down again. But my mind was trawling memories that were ten years old.

'The call had come in at around eight in the evening,' I told her. 'Dark. Sylvia's next-door neighbour had a phone, and, having heard screaming and shouting, followed by a worrying silence from Sylvia's place, she had investigated. As she put it herself, she'd put her head inside Sylvia's front door, which was open, and called out to her. No reply. So she had gone inside to see what was going on. Natural nosiness, though she herself called it concern. The so-called front room was dark, but the door into the rear room, the kitchen, where the light was on—that door was open. After calling out Sylvia's name, and receiving no reply, she had ventured further. She told me her heart had been hammering away.'

Amelia moved on the seat, and clutched at my hand. I squeezed it, then I went on, 'Still calling Sylvia's name, but getting more and more worried, although it was the flooding she was worrying about, she moved slowly into the kitchen. She touched nothing—bless her—just stood and stared. The roaring of the river

34

sounded much louder there, because her husband had their own back door firmly closed. In Sylvia Thomas's house, the terrible din, as the neighbour herself put it, was absolutely terrifying. Sylvia's rear door, wide open to the river, allowed in the full volume of the frightening noise. And the spray. The floor was an inch under water. On the formica-topped table, at that time, was a large piece of pastry, in the process of being rolled out, and the rolling-pin. As this rather intelligent neighbour took a step towards Sylvia Thomas's body, the movement of the floor, which apparently had loose planking, must have rocked the table slightly, because the rolling-pin fell off. She reached for it, but snatched her hand away. She knew she mustn't touch anything, as she had already realised that Sylvia Thomas was probably dead. As she watched, staring at the sprawled figure, cheek on the floor and head tilted sideways, the slightly moving water flowed into Sylvia's open mouth, and out again. This neighbour knew then that Sylvia Thomas was positively dead. She told me, later, that she had, at that moment, reached for support, and a set of her own fingerprints was found impressed in one edge of the pastry. She couldn't tell me whether or not she screamed. If she had, it would not have been heard.'

I paused there, allowing my memory to reconstruct it, one detail at a time.

'Then what did she do?' Amelia asked. Her voice was unsteady.

'She backed out, directly into the arms of her husband, who was, by that time, standing in the open front doorway. Then, at last, she fainted. He carried her into their own house, left her in the care of their teenage daughter, and phoned the police station. You realise what that implied, love? The daughter! Who would want a prostitute living next door, in those circumstances? And that's what Sylvia was. All right . . . so she didn't patrol the streets, looking for custom. She had her diary, which we found, and her list of regulars. But was it more acceptable if she was designated, by her clients, as a mistress? There were five of them, when we tracked them down, and each one was under the impression that he was the only one.'

'But Richard . . .' Amelia was a little flushed in the neck. 'If there were five clients . . . were there also five wives?'

'Four, in fact. One client was a widower. But the point I wished to make was that it was not a very wholesome situation, a teenage girl with a prostitute for a next-door neighbour.'

'Hardly,' Amelia agreed. 'And so?'

'The scene was just as she'd described it, when we arrived. The sergeant and I. Just as I've described it, too.'

Then Amelia was silent. We had unleashed the dogs, and they were nosing the water.

Here, they seemed to decide, it wasn't as good as the water that flowed at the foot of our steep garden at home. In any event, they didn't plunge into it.

'You said,' Amelia ventured thoughtfully, 'that the evidence against Connie Freeman was overwhelming. Quite frankly, I've heard nothing yet that indicated—let alone proves—that she was there that evening. It *was* evening, you said?'

'Yes, and it was pitch black outside, with that terrible downpour of rain. The visibility, away from the houses, couldn't have been more than four or five feet.'

'So . . . what connected Connie with the situation . . . with the killing? Overwhelming, you told me.' She was clearly not intending to let it alone. 'I've heard no such evidence yet.'

I sighed, and concentrated on filling my pipe. 'There'd been warnings, you see, love, going on for a month or more, before the actual death. Nothing violent or noisy; no fingers being waved beneath noses in the pub. Sylvia Thomas had half a dozen or so clients, as I told you. The number varied. Sometimes, she and one of them would drive into town— Sylvia preferred the Cromwell Arms, in High Town. And our Connie began to appear there, usually on her own, apart from any casual friends she might meet. Sometimes with her husband, Harry. A bit embarrassing that'd be, for Harry. His wife and his mistress staring at each other across the saloon bar. Then, one evening, about a month before the storm, Connie was in there alone. No escort. I don't know where Harry was—perhaps he was getting too nervous of sitting all evening with his wife smouldering beside him. One of our constables was in there, off duty and therefore not in uniform. At around ten o'clock an old friend of ours, a petty crook, who worked on the edge of crime, not fully into it . . . well . . . he strolled in, looked around, and took his glass to join Connie at her table. Of course, our man became interested at this point, and kept a very casual but careful eye on the situation. They had a couple of drinks, Connie and her man not appearing to be more than acquaintances, and then he, half on his feet and seeming about to leave, drew a bunched handkerchief out of his pocket, put it down on the table, nodded, and left. She'd slipped him an envelope, which had disappeared into his inside pocket. Connie was careful to make sure that Sylvia didn't miss a second of this scene. In fact, we believed, when the loose knots of the evidence were being pulled tight, that it had all been rehearsed.'

Amelia tugged at my sleeve. 'Is this getting anywhere, Richard?'

'Yes,' I said. 'We're there now. It was the beginning of the frightening phase—the handing over of the pistol.'

'A pistol!'

'Yes, love. Wrapped in the handkerchief. Connie allowed Sylvia Thomas to get just a glimpse of it—and there'd have been a cold, warning smile, I expect. Then she made a habit of appearing in any saloon bar that Sylvia patronised, searching around all the pubs, if necessary, and again allowing Sylvia the glimpse. But it didn't work. Sylvia was not so easily scared. And so, as we reconstructed it, Connie became so frustrated that she decided on a visit to Sylvia's house. And perhaps it progressed from threat to actual violence. That, in any event, was how we saw it. A meeting face to face, and it went too far. The rolling-pin was there . . . to hand. What more natural than that Connie should grab it up . . . and use it?'

'So her fingerprints would be on it,' Amelia said, nodding.

I grinned at her. 'No. It had fallen on to the waterlogged floor and the flour on it would've prevented any decent prints from being developed by the forensic team anyway. And . . . Connie normally wore driving gloves. So we couldn't expect to discover any of her prints on the rolling-pin. And we didn't.'

'I'm finding it difficult to imagine,' Amelia said ruefully. 'Are we getting anywhere with all this? You still haven't even mentioned any evidence that Connie *did* go to Sylvia's place that evening.'

'There was evidence,' I assured her. 'Bits

and pieces we managed to put together.'

'Then tell me about your bits and pieces,' Amelia asked, nodding severely.

'Well . . .' I said. 'It was like this. First there were all those threats against Sylvia, which Connie was observed making. When they had no effect Connie visited Sylvia at her home, and the threats became action. Violent action. I'll explain . . .'

I had to pause there. With so much to be told, I needed to organise it in my mind. Amelia said, 'Sticks and stones . . . you know that . . . breaking bones. We used to chant it, when I was little. Now it's words—from you, Richard. Harmless words.'

'All right,' I said. 'Facts, then.' And I plunged in.

'When we got there, Sylvia was lying face down—as I said—with her arms stretched out in front of her, her shoulder wedging open the rear door, and she was wearing a watch on her left wrist. It was a new watch, and we later found out that it had been a present from Harry. It was her birthday, of all days, and on the face of the glass there was a print of Connie's thumb . . .'

'In all that wet?' Amelia protested.

'You'd be surprised what the forensic wizards can do. Yes, they did manage to develop it, and it was pointing—the thumbprint —in the direction of Sylvia's elbow. Exactly how it would've been if Connie had gripped both wrists and pulled Sylvia across the floor, with the intention of throwing her outside into the flood, but just couldn't find enough strength to manage that final act. If she'd succeeded, it would've been a perfect murder, because when Sylvia's body was eventually found—and heaven knows how long that would have taken—it would have been so battered around that a blow to the head wouldn't have been detected as being deliberate.'

But Amelia was shaking her head, stubbornly rejecting my scenario.

'Do you seriously expect me to believe that?' she demanded. 'Don't tell me she admitted it. One minute you say that there were no fingerprints on the rolling-pin, because of the flour on it, and possibly because Connie was wearing her driving gloves. Now— all of a sudden—you say that Connie's thumbprint was on the watch-glass. Am I supposed to accept that she carefully removed her gloves, just to make sure she put a thumbprint on the watch? Oh . . . come *on*, Richard. This is sounding like a farce.'

I shrugged. 'Nevertheless, there was the thumbprint. So there was evidence that she'd tried to throw Sylvia out into the flood.'

'A thumbprint!' she said, as though that could be bizarre. 'And in all that wet, too! Did she admit that?'

'She admitted nothing,' I told her. 'Nothing

at all. She said she had intended to go there, that evening, to give Sylvia Thomas a piece of her mind, but the weather was absolutely terrible, and when she got to the parking patch—the one we used—her Volks began to feel as though she'd never get going again if she left it there, the surface being nothing but mud, so she turned it round while she'd still got a bit of a grip with the tyres, and drove home—promising herself that she'd go there on another evening, when the weather was better.'

'And?' asked Amelia, obviously feeling that I hadn't finished it.

'Nothing more.' I shrugged. 'Just that fact— that she turned the car round while she still had it moving, and drove away.'

Amelia shook her head. She was concentrating on her own thoughts. 'And the gun?' she asked.

'Well,' I explained, 'it was just a frightener. It was a plastic toy. And for the past three or four weeks Connie had haunted Sylvia, spying on her. Whoever she was with—in whatever pub in town—as long as it wasn't with her husband, with Harry—there was Connie, watching Sylvia, smiling meaningfully at her and patting her shoulder bag. But it didn't work. Sylvia let it slide right past her, and continued as she'd been doing before, which was enough to infuriate Connie into tactics a little more violent. So we reasoned it, anyway.

There was no mention from either Connie or Harry, when we got down to the serious interrogations, of the bitter rows they must have had at home.'

Amelia grimaced at the thought.

'The first actual act of violence,' I went on, 'must have been that visit on the night of the storm. The weather was possibly a help to Connie, as her black Beetle would have been virtually invisible on the parking patch. But one of the neighbours, arriving home in his own car, walked into it. A black car on a black evening. He told us he'd had the impression that it was a Volkswagen Beetle. It was weak evidence, but it was helpful to us.'

'Not good for Connie,' Amelia said, frowning as she considered it.

'Not good at all,' I agreed. 'We simply didn't believe what she claimed, which was that she'd turned around and driven away. She'd previously said that she'd parked in a lay-by, but she finally conceded that she'd driven on to that parking patch, only a hundred yards from the row of houses, but didn't stop. If she did drive there in such terrible weather—and it was a good three miles from her home—it indicated that she had serious and determined intentions. She wouldn't have been discouraged, when she was so close to achieving what she had in mind.'

Amelia grimaced. 'She was trying to frighten a prostitute. Almost impossible, I'd have thought. All prostitutes must be as tough as nails, and after all, sexual assault could easily become actual physical assault. They do lay themselves open to it.'

'One way of putting it,' I agreed. 'In fact, they rarely encounter violence.'

'Hmm!' She lifted her eyebrows. 'They can always shout for a policeman, I suppose. *Do* the police protect them, Richard?'

'Well . . . unofficially. They do a public service, you see. A rejected client might easily turn into a determined rapist. Or vice versa. What the police officially object to is the women patrolling the streets, and men in cars driving around to pick them up.'

'What strange ideas you have, Richard. You surprise me.'

I shrugged. 'It's a point of view. But of course, when the situation involves a wife . . . well, for Connie, the very fact that Sylvia wasn't impressed by a pistol, which looked real enough . . . that must have been the last straw. Connie would have been sufficiently infuriated to look round for stronger tactics than an empty threat. So we reasoned it, back at the station. And the first violent tactic was that visit on the night of the storm. Connie must have worked herself into quite a fury even to have ventured out in that weather. But, I suppose, there's always a breaking point, and then the storm would not have put her off. And I wouldn't have been surprised if she'd admitted that she'd forced her way into Sylvia's house. Then the stage would have been set for almost anything, if both of them lost all vestiges of their self-control. Perhaps Sylvia Thomas laughed at her. Maybe Connie's reaction to that was rather more forceful than Connie had intended, and she found herself with the body of Sylvia Thomas to deal with, but she hadn't got the physical strength to dispose of her by throwing her out of the door and into the flood. Only to drag her across the floor. And that's how it was: the case against Connie Martin, who now calls herself Freeman and could hardly care less about Harry's activities.'

Amelia was silent for a few moments, until we turned away and called the dogs to heel, and attached their leads. Then she said, 'And that's it?' She didn't sound enthusiastic.

'That's it,' I agreed. 'Not, to my mind, a dead solid case, but the jury brought in a guilty verdict.'

'So, what do you intend to do about it?' she asked. 'What *can* you do to help Connie?'

'Well . . . I don't know,' I had to admit. 'I suppose—visit the people who were involved. Talk to them, and try to revive their memories. Perhaps something will emerge. Something I missed.'

'Hmm!' She frowned. 'It's all perhaps. Not very optimistic, are you, Richard?'

'It's that thumbprint on the watch-glass I

can't get round.'

'Oh . . . that!' Amelia dismissed it with a flick of her hand. 'It doesn't mean a thing.'

I stared at her. It had been the centrepiece of my case, my only positive evidence that Connie had been inside Sylvia's house. The prosecuting counsel had made a major issue of it, and Amelia was calmly dismissing it!

'It means,' I said, 'or rather it meant to me at that time, that Connie had been in Sylvia's house that evening—and more than likely found herself laughed at. And that would have pushed her over the edge, from heated dispute to actual violence. There comes a time, you know, in this kind of situation, when rational thought gets thrown out of the window, and only some sort of positive action seems to be reasonable. Any action . . . such as grabbing for the nearest available weapon, and lashing out. And there she'd be, with a dead woman lying at her feet, and struggling to control herself while trying to decide what to do about it. So . . . the only action reasonable enough to contemplate would have been an attempt to throw the body out into the river, which, it seemed, she had tried to do.'

Amelia smiled; to herself, really. 'I thought you said the watch was a birthday present from Harry.'

It was obvious that Amelia had something to throw at me, and was even enjoying the anticipation.

'Well . . . yes.' I was cautious about that. It could lead into irrelevancies.

There was a wicked gleam in Amelia's eyes. 'Imagine . . . what if Harry had been fool enough to leave it lying around, in its presentation box, at home. And Connie, intrigued, even perhaps guessing for whom it was intended, had lifted it from its box and gripped it in anger, before replacing it . . . *that* would have produced her thumbprint. Harry took the watch to Sylvia, and he'd have not the slightest idea that it already had Connie's thumbprint on it.'

I was restless, and got up from the bench to walk a few paces. Anybody can produce wild and improbable theories, but I didn't want to start a dispute with Amelia.

'You could be on to something,' I conceded, seating myself again. 'But it's a bit far-fetched.'

'No more so than your own theory, Richard. From a thumbprint, you built up a theory that involved Connie Freeman trying to get rid of Sylvia's body by throwing it into the river.'

I nodded. Grunted. Said nothing.

'But Richard, love,' she said, 'there's still another way her thumbprint could have got on the watch-glass. A quite innocent way.'

'So . . . enlighten me.' And I suppose I shouldn't have smiled, because she flashed back at me.

'The obvious way, Richard! Oh, you *are* slow, sometimes. Yes . . . assume that Connie

47

was there. Yes, she had probably gone along to do a bit more of her frightening act. But . . . suppose, Richard . . . just consider this. If Connie got there and found Sylvia Thomas lying, apparently dead, where you found her— what would have been her first reaction? I'll tell you. It would have been almost instinctive. She'd have gone to her, crouched down, and felt for a pulse in her wrist. *Then* her thumb would probably have been on the watch-glass, and she'd have had to remove a glove—if she was wearing gloves. And of course, as she'd been making all these threats around the place, she'd have realised how awkward her situation now was . . . and she would get out of there, and away, as fast as she could. Don't you think so, Richard? Don't you?'

And I could do no more than say, 'Yes, love.'

But Connie had said nothing about feeling for a pulse.

CHAPTER THREE

I took a left turn out on to the main road. Then, within half a mile, I turned off into what was clearly a minor road.

'Where are we going now?' Amelia asked. She had been silent for quite a few minutes.

'To see Connie, if she's home. You'll be able to form your own opinion of her.'

But Amelia had probably already formed her opinion of Connie, though one had to allow for the fact that people present a different and more relaxed personality under their own roof.

'How far is it?'

'About a mile, if I remember it correctly,' I told her. 'Perhaps two. We can't miss it. You'll see.'

I registered her nod in the corner of my left eye. No doubt she would be eager to ask Connie a question or two of her own. But she said nothing on this, waiting to see whether I satisfied her reservations with my own questions.

This was a minor road to Ironbridge, and, if my memory was reliable, we would eventually drive between a run of high farmer's hedge on our right-hand side, and on the other side a run of high stone wall, supporting from collapse the front gardens of half a dozen bungalows in proud array, which projected an appearance of wealthy complacency, coupled with an awareness that they were the only habitations visible in any direction. Gracefully, they stood there, convinced of their own superiority.

Of necessity, the drive ran up quite steeply to the frontages and the double garages beside each one of them, whereas the front lawns were flat and level.

Here, you would feel almost ashamed if you managed to survive with only one car per bungalow, and the residents would certainly need their own transport. No public conveyances came this way, as far as I knew. We had certainly seen none.

'The second drive from here,' I said. 'Can't miss it. Trailing roses.'

But it was the wrong time of the year for the splendid floral display enjoyed by this short length of sunken road, as it seemed to be when driving past.

Neighbours clearly competed for the finest effects. Here, you would not find climbing plants. You saw hanging ones, like waterfalls of blazing colour, three feet above your car roof, at times clattering against it and scattering a snowfall of petals, along with their perfume, all over your car.

On the other side of the road was placed a pole, opposite each driveway, all bearing double mirrors facing the houses at angles.

This was to give the residents a chance of driving out into the road without meeting, head on, an unseen vehicle, driven fast by a stranger to the district who might fail to catch a sight of any hint of a drive. The hanging gardens, seen at an acute angle, completely obscured the presence of entrances.

Fortunately, the Freeman household was the only one favouring rambling roses for their waterfalls of colour, the rest being content to rely on geraniums and other trailing plants. In any event, that was the drive I chose. The roses had rambled rather more wildly than I remembered them, and at this time were past their petal-shed, and were covered with red hips.

With a long blast of the horn, I turned in, dropped down a couple of gears, and climbed the steep drive up to the extensive parking area. Each bungalow was surrounded by a more than adequate area of territory, and there was no difficulty in finding room to park.

Two metal-slatted garage doors faced us as I cut the engine. I glanced at Amelia, considering what she would be thinking about the obvious aura of wealth. I knew that to be deceptive, but I said nothing about it.

One of the garage doors was in its up position, and working on a powerful-seeming Suzuki motor cycle were two young people in riding outfits, the visors of their helmets raised. It was a few moments before I realised

51

that one of them was a young woman—
Connie's son's girlfriend. She was holding a
large adjustable spanner, which I guessed had
just slipped from the nut or bolt she was
struggling with and had rapped her thumb.
Her remarks on this occurrence were not at all
ladylike. Connie's son lifted his head and
grinned at me. But it was to his companion
that he spoke.

'Go and put it under the cold-water tap,
Penny,' he said. 'We'll be with you in a couple
of secs.'

She straightened, flicked a grimace of a
smile at me, then hurried away, as close to a
run as her rather restrictive black waterproof
over-trousers would permit. She was heading
round the bungalow for the rear door, in
order, I supposed, to welcome us at the front.

Quite clearly, Connie was not at home, and
these two were at this time in charge. Indeed,
from what Connie had told us, it seemed that
they had been living together here for the best
part of ten years. Connie, if I remembered
correctly, had said that she was well satisfied
with the arrangement. What the girl's parents
felt about it had not been revealed, though it
did occur to me that it was they who must have
kept these two solvent. There had been no
suggestion that Harry, who was, after all,
Philip's father, had helped them financially.

But the situation had meant that Connie's
home had been kept in a reasonable condition.

Lived in.

Philip said, 'If you'll give it a couple of minutes, Penny will let you in at the front door. She likes things to be done correctly and formally.'

'Nice bike,' I said. In my early days as a constable I had been on motor-cycle patrol, so I did know something about them.

'Yeah,' said Philip. 'It runs as smooth as silk. We've covered a lot of miles on this. It's Penny's, really, because her dad bought it for us. I'm teaching her to drive it.'

'Umm!' I said.

This bike was a distinct improvement on the rackety old Triumph twin he had been using at the time of Sylvia Thomas's death. I could recall it now, that flabby saddle, near to collapse, and the sponge rubber pillion with the split covering, which must have been painful for Penny to ride on.

Amelia was looking round appreciatively at the bungalow, the garden, and the other five bungalows comprising the run. No doubt she was wondering why Connie, if she owned such a splendid property, should be running a battered old Beetle. On this aspect of Connie's life, I knew nearly every detail. But it was not the time to explain it all to Amelia; it would take too long, and already she was moving towards the front door.

The fact was that Connie's father, Tony, had built these six bungalows. He had been a

53

small-time builder with large ambitions, and when this parcel of land had come on the market, and no enthusiastic bids were made by local farmers, who looked askance at the steep fall to the road below (at that time guarded only by a rather flimsy hedgerow), Tony stepped in, and spent all his spare cash on the land. Then he set out to build six bungalows, having persuaded his bank manager to let him take a risk, and to advance the necessary loan, which anybody more experienced (such as Harry) would have told Tony was fraught with dangers. The bungalows were perhaps too isolated. They were also rather expensive. They did not sell very well, certainly not fast enough to keep level with the interest on the bank's loan, which mounted in steps with too many naughts at the end. And Tony found himself in financial trouble. Perhaps he had failed to allow for the loss of income from the bungalow he gave to Connie. Or perhaps he had not allowed for the expensive concrete and rock wall, which proved to be necessary, and indeed compulsory, in order to support the front gardens from collapse on to the road below. Or both of these.

In any event, he never built another house, was declared bankrupt, and quietly drank himself to death.

So Connie was left with a bungalow much too large for her, and which she could not really afford to maintain, inconveniently located more than two miles from the nearest public transport (and that very infrequent). She had no income, because her life had rotated around the continuing welfare of her beloved father, who had persisted, in spite of all her pleas, threats and curious attacks on his character, in steadily drinking his life away. A small insurance pay-out enabled her to buy the Volkswagen Beetle, which was necessary, as she needed transport if she intended not to abandon her bungalow. But it had been built especially for her, and by her father, to include her own personal requirements. How, then, could she part with it?

Certainly, she had needed financial advice, so she consulted an accountant. His name was Harry Martin, and he apparently advised her to marry someone who knew how to wangle financial matters. As he was the only one in her sphere of acquaintances who clearly did know how to wangle such things, she eventually married him, with the eager optimism of a woman blinded by his charm, which later proved to be superficial.

The marriage turned out to be a mistake. They had one child—Philip—whom Harry virtually ignored. Philip, to Harry, was a nuisance, who attracted Connie's attention far too much of the time; Harry thrived on attention, as long as it was complimentary, and expected more than his fair share of adulation.

But Connie's affection for Harry,

diminished by the love she showered on Philip, gradually died away, and from then onwards Harry looked around him, and began to derive more comfort and sexual satisfaction from casual pick-ups. Until he met Sylvia Thomas, when it became rather more than casual, so that his marriage subsided into being no more than a mockery, and a minor issue in his life—an opinion shared by Connie, although she always felt deeply hurt by his philandering.

And then Sylvia Thomas died, on that terrible evening of the storm and the flooded Severn, and the cohesion of the whole family broke apart with Connie's arrest for murder. I was the one who made the arrest.

All this, Connie had told me at the time of her detention, when we had become enwrapped in her bouts of interrogation, and before she was charged with the murder of Sylvia Thomas. Hours we spent, talking together. Most of what she told me was quite irrelevant to Sylvia Thomas's death, but I encouraged her to talk about what the background had been. It seemed to relax her, to be able to talk about it freely to a stranger. But not a word of it helped in the defence. Harry's exploits with Sylvia Thomas amounted only to a small added wound to Connie's already hurt pride. But it can be the smallest of wounds that will bring you down, unless treated. That, I was certain, was what had happened. The treatment. Connie, I believed, had taken decisive action. Convinced, at that time, of her guilt, I charged her, but with the mental reservation that I was surprised she hadn't also killed her husband, Harry. And first.

But I didn't say that to her at the time, though maybe the opportunity might shortly arise, I thought, if I could work my way round to it.

In the meantime, I put a thumb on the front door bell-push, and heard the bell's double chime from somewhere far down the hall.

'We don't know how long Connie might be,' said Amelia.

'Could be home any minute, perhaps,' I suggested hopefully.

'Umm! Perhaps.'

Then the door opened to reveal a young woman whom, for a few seconds, I failed to recognise as Philip's friend, who had been helping him with some unspecified trouble with the motor bike.

She had worked fast, discarding the motor-cycling togs, and now seemed decidedly feminine, in spite of the jeans and the denim jacket, with a waterfall of wildly untidy auburn hair, and the makings of a pout, possibly in apology for Connie's absence. But her lips looked as if they were more used to smiling, and the brown eyes gleamed, cheeks chubbily red from the cool wind outside, and possibly from the effort required for wielding the large adjustable spanner I had seen her handling. She seemed not to use much in the way of make-up, possibly because of the work she had been doing on the bike, and her lips were having difficulty in maintaining a fixed absence of anything resembling a welcoming smile. Yet it was there, that smile and welcome, there in her eyes and the toss of her hair.

'You'd better come in,' she said, frowning as she considered the exact extent of welcome to offer. It was not her bungalow; she was not its mistress. 'She's just nipped into Ironbridge. Won't be long. Can you come back . . . or . . .'

'We'd rather wait, if you don't mind, and if she's not to be too long,' said Amelia. 'It's not terribly important—is it, Richard?'

As I hadn't the faintest idea about what I might ask Connie, and was hoping that inspiration would appear when required, all I could say was, 'Not really.'

Then a male voice intervened. 'Oh, come on in. You can surely wait for a few minutes, can't you! She won't be long, and . . .'

There he stopped. I could see now that he, too, had stepped out of his riding kit—in the kitchen, I guessed.

He had been walking towards us along the hall, unable to see us very well, and obviously he had not paid us much attention outside. Now he had a clear view, as the young lady had stepped back to his side, and was hugging his arm. At once, Philip remembered.

58

'Here . . . I know you,' he said. 'You're that copper who did all the questioning. That night! Yeah . . . I remember you—couldn't forget. You'd better come inside and sit down. But . . . that night!' he repeated. 'I'll never forget it. It's been sort of haunting me ever since . . . if you know what I mean. Lord! the rain we had!'

He had been speaking with a certain amount of intimacy, as though we had shared an adventure.

'You'd better come in,' he repeated, rather doubtfully, I thought. 'If you can wait,' he added.

'Oh . . . we can wait,' said Amelia. 'We're in no hurry.'

And the young woman stood aside, her smile very close to being a grimace. Then she turned, and walked back down the hall. There was reluctance in her attitude: she did not want us there, and she left me to close the front door.

From behind, although she was not tall and seemed quite small-boned, there was a wiry sturdiness about her bearing and I could imagine that she would have no difficulty in driving Philip's motor cycle. In fact, there was something of the tomboy about her, I thought—apart from the hip swing. She was well aware that I was a mature man. But it was her face that I found attractive. There had been humour and intelligence in her eyes.

59

Now, she no longer made any attempt to swing her hips. She was expressing a total lack of interest in me.

'In here,' said Philip, standing back for his girlfriend to slide past him. I saw her raise a hand, and allow one finger to slide over his lips. Could she possibly, I thought, be warning him to be careful about what he said?

He left us sufficient room to enter, stood back to allow us to pass him, then closed the door. I looked around the room as the girl offered an easy chair to Amelia, who smiled, but shook her head.

It was a huge room, Connie's father no doubt believing that big was beautiful. But it did produce the effect that much more furniture was needed if a feeling of isolation were to be averted. It was their front room, their sitting-room by my definition, and the wide, handsome bay window offered a splendid view over farmland stretching to the horizon, with the hills squatting beyond and mist drifting in the distant valleys.

Connie's father had obviously paid special attention to this bungalow, intended in his mind for Connie. The mahogany panelling, to a height of six feet from the floor, must have been expensive, and even the pictures hanging against the panels seemed costly, though they must have been prints, mainly of the Impressionists' works. The bay window was curtained with a heavy plush material, the lights were affixed to the walls in three-branch outlets, and the three-piece suite, even with the support of sundry extra easy chairs and a large, round table, still left a considerable area of empty space.

'I'm Philip,' the young man introduced himself. 'In case you don't remember me. I remember you, all right. You were in charge of everything when that, that . . . tart, Sylvia Thomas, got herself killed.'

'We didn't think she caused it herself,' I said mildly, trying to smile but not succeeding. He had gone straight to the heart of it, recognising me so easily. It seemed that, even after ten years, the death of Sylvia Thomas still occupied a position well to the front of his mind.

He had been only about sixteen at that time, but it was an age at which he, and this young woman, had felt sufficiently mature to take over the bungalow, to look after it for Connie, as they had no doubt justified it to themselves. I wondered what her parents had thought about that.

'I'll go and brew us a pot of tea,' said the girl, demonstrating her authority under his roof.

'No, no,' put in Amelia quickly, knowing that I would prefer to have the girl there, where I could watch her reactions.

'I would like to ask you both a few questions,' I explained to her, smiling, trying to ease the tension in the air. 'I'm not in the police now, it's just me, with no official backing. Me. Unofficial. You can tell me to get the hell out of here, if you like. And Philip could back you up—and I'd go. But, you see, it's Connie who's asked me to get involved again, and I don't think she'd be too pleased if we didn't hang on here for a while, until she returns.'

Though I had said this in a very mild way, she seemed rather more disconcerted than the situation justified.

'Yes, Penny,' said Philip. 'No need for any fuss. Oh . . . this is Penny Downes. Mr and Mrs Patton. There, I've remembered your name! Fancy that. It came out of nowhere. It's all right, Penny. He's on our side—or so it seems to me.' He produced a special smile for Amelia. 'And your wife, of course.'

I had not considered myself to be on anybody's side, even though it had been Connie who had asked me to take another look at the case. All that was carrying me forward into this investigation was an uncertainty. For my own peace of mind, I now had to see it through.

But the thought had occurred to me that it might be a good idea to try a few questions on these two. It would, at least, fill in the time. But I realised that I would have to be cautious.

'Your mother,' I told Philip, 'was quite adamant, when she came to visit us, that she was not at Sylvia Thomas's place on that terrible evening. We—the police—had reason to believe she *was* there.' I didn't intend to discuss with him the flimsy evidence of the thumbprint on the watch-glass. 'She was there, Philip. We were certain of that,' I told him, watching his growing frown of disbelief—or of concern.

'I know she was,' he said quietly, at last.

'You *know*?' There had been so much calm certainty in his voice that the words burst from me.

'Yes!' He snapped it out.

'How can you possibly know? Has she said that? No . . . wait.' I held up my palm. 'Before you say another word, I'll have to remind you that I'm not talking as a policeman, now. I'm just a civilian, trying to get to the truth.'

And what I had thought to be the truth—if I were to believe Connie—was slipping from me with what Philip had already said.

He allowed himself a cynical smile. Penny slid her hand into his. Her eyes were wide, startled. But this could surely not be new to her. Philip must have told her about it. If he intended their relationship to be in any way lasting, he would have had to take her into his confidence. And it *had* lasted. They had, it seemed, lived together in this bungalow for the best part of ten years.

Philip kissed her on the forehead, and she flickered a smile at him.

'Well . . .' he said, turning to me. 'If you're after the truth—though I can't see what good that'll do you—you'll have to accept that my mother *was* there, and she *did* go to Sylvia Thomas's place. And she was missing for a good five minutes. At least. I got away from the Beetle smart-like, when I saw her torchlight coming my way. I knew it was my mother coming back for her car, but I didn't want to meet her—talk to her—didn't want her to find out that I knew all about dad and that Sylvia creature. So I kept out of the way till she'd gone, then I got on my bike and left.'

Then he smiled complacently, clearly proud of himself.

This was all new to me, yet he was speaking with confidence, assuming that I already knew the basics of it. The words had tumbled from his lips. As though he had rehearsed it to himself, and could no longer contain them.

There had not been any suggestion, at that time, that Philip was in any way involved in the death of Sylvia Thomas. I had, I recalled, dismissed him from my mind, when I had heard he was only sixteen. But now he seemed almost too eager to supply me with facts and implications, and I had to remind myself that sixteen-year-olds were capable of anything.

All I could think to do—to say—was to stall for time. My mind was chasing around madly, trying to slot this in.

'You were fifteen or sixteen at the time,' I

said, probing. 'What about licence and insurance, and the like? For that bike of yours?'

'Ha!' he said. 'I had to manage without, didn't I!'

My reaction to this was that of a policeman, appalled at what I had heard, lining up in my mind the laws Philip had broken. But then I controlled my instincts as being paltry. Why should I worry? I was no longer a policeman.

'And you followed your mother to the place—'

I wanted to tie him down to details, details I hadn't extracted at that time, but he cut in with a brisk gesture of his hand, then turned away to look out of the window.

'Not followed,' he said. 'Not my mother, not really. Followed my dad, sort of. From memory. Oh . . . I knew where *he* went. I'd followed him before. Twice. Him in that Land Rover of his.' Then he turned back to face me. 'Couldn't believe it. Just couldn't. But there was my mother, on that bloody terrible evening—my mother, in her Beetle, heading in the same direction. Had me worried, that it did. I hated every bit of it, Mr Patton. Hated it—and all I was thinking was that I could've . . . in some way or other . . . I don't know how . . . but I thought I'd be able to sort of put the mockers on it. You know how it is. He'd be ashamed if I turned up, I reckoned. But—as I said—my mother was there ahead of me.'

He turned back from the window, and grimaced at Penny. So very long, Philip had lived with this secret, which had done nothing but ferment—the wound had never healed, and was still giving him pain. Yet surely, Penny must have known all about it, and for a long while. Nevertheless, he seemed to be apologising to her, and was attempting to put that apology into words, justifying himself.

'I felt rotten, Penny,' he said, turning to her. 'That I did. As you'd know.'

She nodded solemnly, and tried to smile.

'I was a sort of peeping Tom,' he went on. 'A . . . there's a French word for it.'

'Voyeur,' she offered, whispering.

'Yeah . . . that.'

'But your mother was there first?' I asked cautiously. At any moment he might realise he was telling me too much, that he was undermining his mother's claim to innocence.

'Well . . . yes,' he said.

'Did you see her? Inside the house, perhaps? Or going inside, or coming out?'

'No. Not her,' he said dully.

'Then . . . who?'

He shook his head, shrugged, and glanced at Penny, almost in apology. 'When it came to it,' he said, 'I couldn't do it. I'd had the idea I'd go along the river path, and walk in on them. But as you know, Mr Patton, it was just downright impossible.'

So he knew about that river path. How?

Had he been there before? Yes, he had said something about that. Twice, he'd said. How could he have known about it, anyway, except by following his father, as it seemed he had eventually done? But now we were talking about that one special evening, when it had been his mother, not his father, whom he had been following.

The thought whispered through my mind that Connie, too, must have been there before. She had said nothing about it, at the time.

Yet it had been a terrible evening, almost impossible to contend with on a motor cycle, I would have thought.

'You couldn't have walked along the river path,' I agreed, 'so I suppose you had to go to the front door, and—'

'No!' he cut in. 'The whole thing was a botch-up. I didn't *see* my mother. Didn't see her at any time, there. Hell, you know what the weather was like. Next to no visibility. How could I dare to go to the front door? Anyway, when it came to it, I just packed it in and came away, after a bit of a snoop around. Nothing to see, though. Rain like a waterfall. Nothing to see,' he repeated. 'So I went back for my bike.'

'So you couldn't even be certain that it *was* your mother who had driven there? It was a hell of a night—that rain!'

Philip glanced at Penny, shrugging, grimacing his displeasure at involving her in this way. Perhaps he hadn't already told her about that terrible evening, and about the death of Sylvia Thomas. If not, he would certainly now have to tell her the full story, in detail, if their relationship were to prosper. I thought he realised that, because he reached for her hand. She flashed a smile at him.

'You couldn't even have been sure your mother *was* there,' I persisted.

'Oh yes I could. Her Beetle was parked on that rotten patch. Just mud, it was, that evening.'

'How could you know it was hers?' I demanded, trying to dent his confidence. 'It could have been just another Volkswagen Beetle. There were a lot of them around, at that time, and most of them black.'

'It was hers.'

'Something special about it, was there? Something different from all the others? Number plate, if you could see it.'

'It was hers. After I'd walked part of the way to the row of houses, and it wasn't all that easy—the mud I had to plod through! Anyway, I reckoned it was all hopeless, a dead waste of time, so I came back—went back—for my bike, and got away from there.' He hesitated, then added, 'After my mother had driven off. The bike seat was soaking wet, and the pillion seat worse, because it was sponge, with the cover worn all thin.'

None of this accorded with what Connie herself had said—that she had turned away without stopping.

'Hmm!' I said doubtfully. There had been no mention of this when I had spoken to him at that time. 'The weather . . .' It had dominated our conversation. 'How the devil could you have known it *was* your mother's car?'

I had already asked him this, and his reply hadn't been satisfactory. A black car and a black night . . .

'Yeah,' he said. 'But it wasn't all that tricky. Me . . . I'd got there, but I couldn't leave the bike. You know what that so-called parking patch was like. It was just hopeless, trying to lean the bike on its prop-stand. Sank into the mud, it did. So . . . well, there was the Volks, so I leaned the bike against it, on the passenger side, then when I got back . . .'

'Not having seen any proof, nothing positive, that it *was* your mother you'd been chasing?'

'Oh . . . come on!' he protested. 'I'd seen her drive off from home. From here. I just followed.'

'But not too close,' I suggested. 'Or she would've realised it could be you.'

He shook his head, gave a glance at Penny, as much as to say, 'The man's stupid,' sighed, and said, 'She'd just have seen a headlight. I didn't hang on her tail. I'm not that stupid. Fell back, then closed up, and so on. I had a damned good idea where she was heading, anyway.'

'So—all right,' I conceded. 'You followed the Beetle to that parking patch. But you wouldn't have had anything to prove to yourself that it *was* your mother's car parked there, a black car and with the visibility down to about a yard or so. You couldn't see the number plate. It could have been anybody's.'

He stared at me, turned to Penny, winked at her, displaying his confidence, then turned back to me. 'I couldn't prop up the bike,' he explained. 'I've *told* you that. So I leaned it against the Beetle, passenger side, and you can guess . . . it slid when the car drove away, and it was on its side when I got back to it.' He shrugged. 'So there it is. The facts.'

He was eyeing me with anxiety. Amelia jerked at my elbow, prompting a response.

'It doesn't prove anything,' I told Philip, sighing. 'There were a lot of black Beetles around, at that time. How could you possibly be certain it was your mother's?'

He grinned. 'Easy. I told you—I leaned the bike against it, and, when it slid off, my brake lever must've scored the door panel. And there it was, the next day, the score all across the passenger's door, and bits of black paint on my front brake lever. D'you want any better proof than that?'

I glanced at Amelia, but she didn't intend to help me out with this. This lad—man, now; he was twenty-six, Connie had said—this young

70

man was deliberately attempting to strengthen the evidence against his own mother. But there had been no mention of this at the time of the investigation. So . . . why now? Was it that he wanted me to go away with the impression that I had been quite correct, at that time, with my arrest of his mother? And thus leave him in peace?

If that were the case, then it began to appear that he had something to hide, which could only mean that he was more closely involved in Sylvia Thomas's death than I had previously thought. But I dared not pounce on this point in case I scared him off, in which event he would retreat into a defensive stance and I would get nothing more out of him.

Penny said abruptly, 'She ought to be back by now. We'd have had plenty of time for a cup of tea, after all.'

Philip had moved to the window, anxious for his mother to return. To rescue him, I thought. He had perhaps heard himself saying things he ought to have suppressed. Or things that were untrue?

'She's here now,' he said abruptly. 'I'll go and let her in.' And he almost ran into the hall.

This was clearly unnecessary, as I heard her key in the lock before he could have reached the door. There were mumbled, quick words between them in the hall, then she swept in.

'You've brought your dogs, I see,' she greeted us. 'I'm so glad. You needn't have left

71

them in the car, you know.'

The fact that she was carrying a dog basket, with two objects inside, which might or might not have been dogs (as they were rolling around in one ball of tangled fur) did not surprise me. She had said she intended to acquire a dog. It seemed that she had acquired two. Had one of our dogs—or better both—been brought in earlier, and off their leads, I could imagine the chaos that would have ensued.

'Haven't I always told you, Philip?' said Connie. 'Haven't I? That a dog—or better still, two dogs—left in your car is the best anti-theft device ever invented. I've always done that. Aren't they lovely?' she asked, lifting open the lid.

Philip made no response. They were two golden cocker spaniels—puppies. Replacements for the two that Harry had had put down. And then I realised why Philip was being so silent. It was not so much that he didn't get along with dogs. Rather, it was a reminder to him that, at the time when he had—he'd claimed—leaned his motor bike against the door of his mother's Beetle, Connie's two cockers, subsequently put down by Harry, would have been in her Beetle. She would not have travelled without them. And they would have barked their heads off if someone they knew, one of the family had gone to the passenger's door, with the apparent intention of allowing them their freedom to chase after Connie, and then had denied them that privilege. Philip had forgotten that. Or rather, he had not realised that it would have happened, and thus had not mentioned it. Therefore, he had informed me that he had been lying. So . . . had he not, then, followed his mother there? Had he, in fact, been there at all? If so, he had made a proper botch of his cover-up.

He had clearly not read his Sherlock Holmes.

'Oh God, Ma! Not more dogs!' he said.

The two golden cocker pups were chasing each other like mad things all around the room and over the furniture.

'Aren't they lovely!' said Connie.

Nobody added a word.

CHAPTER FOUR

After the dogs had calmed down, and indicated an interest in food and water, Connie took them out to her kitchen to satisfy them. Philip and Penny seemed to be uneasy, and after a rapid, whispered interchange of words, they agreed on something or other that I couldn't understand, and went in search of Connie. That was the last we saw of them, apart from through the window. They had apparently agreed that there was urgent business to be dealt with elsewhere, as we saw them, now again clad in riding gear, walk out to the Suzuki. They looked very alike, in their outfits, except that Penny's canvas shoulder bag was thumping against her hip, and, unlike Philip, she wore leggings and not full over-trousers.

Connie came in as we watched them ride away. She said, 'They'll be going to her mother's.'

'Oh yes?' said Amelia.

'The mother seems to approve of Philip.' But Connie didn't sound certain.

'Just as well, perhaps,' I suggested. 'They make a good-looking pair.'

'Yes.' Connie still sounded uneasy. 'If looks are all that matters.' She was making herself busy by tidying the chair cushions.

74

'You're not happy with it?' Amelia suggested, as we had got on to a subject in which she could express interest.

Connie shrugged. 'Oh . . . I'm quite pleased with the idea. I like the girl. We get on well together, but . . . you know how it is. Two women under the same roof: it just doesn't work. And Penny's sometimes a little bossy. It seems such a pity. Here I am, with all this floor space around me, and only too happy to have them both here. But . . . her mother has what she calls reservations. What she means, really, is that she doesn't like the idea of her precious little darling living under the same roof as an ex-convict. Perhaps she thinks it'll rub off, that I'll train her in pocket-picking, or straight theft from self-service stores, or even . . . how to protect a husband from the evil clutches of another woman. Or . . . take it to the obvious conclusion: how to dispose of that woman.'

She had said this in a flat and toneless voice, but behind her attempt at casualness there had been a deep, painful bitterness.

Amelia laughed, an empty and almost embarrassed laugh. 'Oh . . . come on, Connie, she can't actually have said such a thing.'

Connie shrugged, frowned, then abruptly smiled, and her face lit up. 'Of course she hasn't. It's just . . . oh, I don't know. Perhaps it all comes from my side of it. You come out of prison, and you're obsessed with the thought that you're walking around looking like an ex-con, and that everybody recognises it. Of course, there are people I know, old friends, who are quite aware that I've been in prison. But they're so very friendly, embarrassingly happy to see me . . . and behind it all there's that hint of reservation. She's done it once; she might do it again. And, I suppose, Penny's parents might be wondering whether I'll be doing it to their precious daughter, keeping my eye open for the opportunity—'

'Oh, come on, Connie,' I cut in sharply. 'This is quite ridiculous.'

'Ridiculous to you—yes. To Amelia—yes. But it's there. I am capable of killing a living human being, that's what they see. But it *is* true, in so far as I've learned inside. I can, now, kill a full-grown man, and without a weapon. I know how to do it. Call it self-defence, if you like. And I'm afraid of myself. I *am*, Richard. Don't look at me like that. I've spent nine years in prison, for a murder I didn't do. I'm owed a life. To even things up. Do you think that those nine years might have affected my brain? No doubt they have. But there it is, nudging at me, telling me that I'm owed a life. I've paid for one, and I didn't take it. I can't just toss all those nine years into the past, and simply carry on as though nothing's happened. I can't! And Richard . . .' She reached out for my hand, clutched at it as though she might be drowning, then she whispered, 'Richard . . . I'm terrified of what I

76

might do. To somebody.'

'Anybody special in mind?' I asked lightly, trying to convert the suggestion into a jocular comment, far removed from reality.

She shrugged, and laughed harshly. 'Oh . . . you mustn't take me too seriously. It's just the freedom, you see. Not the physical freedom, but the freedom of being able to say anything I like, and not be afraid of the response. They don't have much sense of humour in prisons, not the wardresses, not the inmates. It's deadly serious . . . inside.'

But there were aspects, I knew, that Connie had not mentioned. She was still an active woman, vigorous and self-possessed, whose idea of a pleasant afternoon was to head away with vigorous strides across any available expanse of grassland, with dogs racing around her. This she could now anticipate with quiet pleasure.

I tried for an easy smile. 'But you'll shake it off, Connie. It'll take a little time, but you'll do it. Don't forget, I've known lots of ex-cons. They all react differently, but in no time at all they're back to where they were before they went inside. Older, but perhaps a little wiser.'

'Are you lecturing me, Richard?' she asked, giving me a weary grimace. 'Or . . . perhaps trying to redeem me?'

'You don't need it, Connie,' I assured her. 'Just be your old self, and everything will fall into place.'

'My old self!' She pouted. 'I can't remember *that* Connie. Do you realise that it's going to be quite a struggle, trying to revive my former life?' And she smiled, a bitter, desolate smile.

'It seems to me,' put in Amelia, 'that you're not going to have much trouble at all. You've already moved a number of steps in the right direction. Isn't that the reason for the dogs? You don't need people.'

And Connie leaned forward, took Amelia by the shoulders, and kissed her on the cheek. 'But they're not all like you, my dear.'

'Well . . .' I said. 'I'd better get on with it.'

'With what?' Connie asked.

'What you wanted me to do. Which, if I remember correctly, is to prove that you didn't kill Sylvia Thomas.'

'Oh . . .' she said. 'Oh yes. I'd quite forgotten.' And for a moment she seemed to be bewildered.

'Forgotten all those lovely damages you were going to claim?' I reminded her. 'When I can prove your innocence.' I raised my eyebrows at her. 'If I can.'

But now she seemed less impetuous. 'Well . . . I don't know. It all looks a bit different, now.'

'In what way?'

'I don't need the money. My investments . . . I've just found out they've grown while I've been inside, and I'm not sure that I want . . .' She shrugged.

'Want what?' I insisted. I had to understand her reservations.

'The publicity.'

'Why not?'

She turned away, flicking a hand dismissively. 'It's Philip. He adores that girl of his—Penny. And the publicity, if my innocence was proved . . . it'd be all over the front page of every newspaper in the country. My very own page . . . my life as an innocent in a prison full of crooks. Ha! And her parents would hate it. Their daughter, Penny Downes, linked with the name of Connie Freeman, ex-convict . . .'

'But proved innocent!' I reminded her, though I kept my fingers mentally crossed.

'As though that would matter! My picture on the front pages. My name. My son's name. They couldn't bear to have their precious Penny connected with Philip, my son. And I would be Connie Martin again. No. They wouldn't permit it, and poor Penny—she would have to do what they told her. No possible connection with that Connie Martin, who's had to hide behind her maiden name of Freeman. Do you think that poor girl could stand up straight and oppose her parents? No . . . never. She hasn't got it in her. I've got to think about my son, Richard. Don't you think I've harmed him enough, being in prison for nine years—'

'But if you're proved innocent?' I protested, trying it once again. After all, it had been she who had involved me in this. I hadn't wanted it. But now . . . there was that niggling doubt, implanted in my brain.

She sighed. 'For nine years I've been a convict. Nothing you can do would call back those nine years. Nothing.'

'For God's sake . . . you asked me to try to prove your innocence,' I reminded her, and I heard my voice rising. Exasperation, that's what it was. Didn't she really want it?

'And I'm asking you now,' she went on, 'to forget all about it. Thank you for what you've done . . .'

Had she read my mind? 'I've done nothing,' I insisted.

'You've done a lot, Richard, though you may not realise it. I can, at least, look people in the face now, even if they choose to turn away.'

I searched frantically in my mind for some way of getting through to her. All right . . . she was no longer talking about the damages she might be able to claim. But that wasn't the important factor, not to me now, because I knew more than I had known at the time of the murder of Sylvia Thomas, and because I was frantically clutching on to my self-esteem. Had I really been such an unobservant fool as it was beginning to seem?

'You can now, of course,' I agreed, 'look people in the face, Connie. You've served your sentence. But what about me? I know now that

80

my investigation at the time was terribly flawed. So—whatever you might say—I'm going to have to continue with it. For my own sake.'

'I don't want you to.'

'For myself, Connie. Not for you. I'm being very selfish.'

But she had turned her back to me, and was staring unseeingly from her splendid window. 'I don't understand you.' She shook her head vigorously.

'I'm going to try to retrieve my self-esteem, if you want it put into words,' I said quietly. 'That's not how it is in my mind. Not exactly. Shall we say, quite simply, that I want to fumble my way to the truth. Just for my own self-satisfaction. And it need not affect you at all, Connie. Just think . . . if I eventually discover evidence—fresh to me—that it *was* you who killed Sylvia Thomas, after all, then at least I could relax.'

I tried to look severe, but it seemed that Connie had left her sense of humour behind in her cell.

'Have you gone insane!' she shouted, and from somewhere, out there where our car was waiting, there came an answering, anxious bark.

'I think not, Connie,' I said, serious again now, if that was what she wanted. 'At the moment I'm trying to sort truth from lies, in what I've been hearing. But I'm finding that people are feeling more free with their information, now. It's in the past, and the murder's been paid for, by you, in prison. So people relax. They are likely to tell me things that they hadn't dared to whisper at that time. So . . . for my own satisfaction, I've got to go along with it. Sorry, Connie, but that's how it is. If you'll tell me where I can find Harry—'

'Harry!' she cut in. '*My* Harry?' For some reason that I couldn't understand, she was at once on the defensive.

'Well . . . that Harry, yes. But he's not yours now, is he? You said something about a divorce. Isn't that so, love?' I asked, turning to Amelia.

But Amelia had been left out of things for too long. Her mind had wandered. 'Isn't what so?' she asked, looking from one face to the other for enlightenment.

'That Connie here said she and Harry are divorced.'

'Oh yes . . . yes. She did say that. I remember her saying it.'

Connie was rapidly losing her temper. I put this down to the fact that I'd indicated every intention of continuing the search for the truth. All right—she'd been charged with the murder of Sylvia Thomas, and still declared her innocence, even if she had abandoned her plan of claiming vast damages. It therefore seemed strange that now she should so vigorously attempt to lure me away from further investigation. Did she fear that I would not find fresh evidence of her innocence, but of her guilt? Yet . . . did she need to fear that? She had served her sentence, and she could not be tried twice for the same crime. She could, in effect, flaunt her guilt.

'I *did* tell you that we divorced,' she said heavily, spacing the words, like a wardress's tread along the corridors.

'And that he's now living with someone named Clarke?'

'Yes, yes,' snapped Connie tersely. 'Jean Clarke. Temporarily, I'd expect.'

'Then all I want is for you to tell me where.'

'Why?' she demanded. 'What do you want to know that for?'

'Well . . . naturally . . . to go there and speak to him.'

'Why?'

'There're questions to be answered. Certain details that still trouble me.'

'What questions?' she persisted, determined to discover what I had in mind. 'Perhaps I could answer them for you.'

'I don't know what questions,' I had to admit. But in fact there was one critical question simply shouting out for clarification. Where had Harry been on the evening of Sylvia Thomas's death? Everybody else seemed to have been hovering or lurking in the vicinity of Sylvia Thomas's house. Because of the weather, and the cover it had supplied for anybody in the vicinity, there was every possibility that, on that special evening, Harry Martin's Land Rover could have been parked close against the side of the distant hedgerow, the boundary of the parking patch. Connie's Beetle had been virtually unseen, and she had made no attempt to conceal it—if, indeed, she *had* parked it on that muddy patch—so Harry Martin's Land Rover would have presented no more than an uncertain outline, part of the shrub background.

Oh yes, certainly I had a good reason for a little chat with Harry. After all, it had been Sylvia's birthday, and Harry had given her a new wrist-watch as a birthday present. It was not a great leap of the imagination to suggest to myself that he had taken it round in the evening, despite the ferocity of the weather. This possibility had not presented itself to me at the time, or, if it had, the thought had slid away and not been considered as a clue, except for that thumbprint of Connie's on the glass. And now seemed to be the time to discuss it with Connie.

'What questions?' Connie demanded again. I had perhaps been silent for too long.

'Well . . .' I said. 'One thing—I want to ask Harry whether he was at the house, Sylvia's house, that evening, and if so, did he take her a birthday present, and if so . . . what?' I smiled at Connie, trying to soften a very severe grimace she gave me.

'You know damn well he was there—and why he wasn't giving evidence in the witness box I can't imagine,' said Connie. 'The watch, you damned fool. Didn't you raise a fuss about it?'

'Of course I did. Connie, you *must* remember this. My question at the time, in court, or rather, the QC's question, was how your thumbprint came to be on that watch when Sylvia had acquired it only that day. You wouldn't answer. You talked all round it. But now . . . why not tell me, Connie? It can't do any harm, now. *Did* you grab hold of her wrist? Did you try to—'

'No, blast you. No! I didn't try to throw her out into the river. I did *not*. The same as I didn't kill her. And if I didn't hit her with that rolling-pin—which I didn't—I wouldn't have *needed* to throw her out into the river. So there!'

'So you didn't grip her wrist—'

'No, no and no!'

'Not even to feel for a pulse?'

'No! How many more times!'

'You didn't *need* to feel for a pulse, I suppose, because you knew you'd hit her hard enough, with that rolling-pin, to kill her in a flash. No need to feel—'

'What the hell's going on here!' she demanded. Then she turned to Amelia. 'What's he supposed to be doing? I ask you. You ought to know. Where's the sense in it?'

85

Amelia tried one of her better smiles, in order to reassure Connie. It had no effect whatsoever.

'What's going on, Connie,' I said, 'is that I'm trying desperately to make sense of a small detail—and you must remember it from the trial—one that's still worrying me. You wouldn't tell me then, and I suppose you're not going to tell me now.'

'So . . . what? What?'

'How did your thumbprint get on the glass face of the watch Sylvia was wearing? In court, you simply said you didn't know. But it won't do, Connie. There had to be a reason. And it matters.'

She was silent . . . shook her head.

'Connie? Please . . .'

Then she looked up, directly into my eyes, and continued quite quietly. 'I didn't tell the truth . . . not all of it. Kept it to myself. I was ashamed for him! For myself, too, I suppose. And you can bet that Harry wouldn't admit it. It was her birthday. You know that. And he'd bought her a watch. There were two watches, there in his briefcase. I heard them rattling around inside when he tossed it on the settee, before he went upstairs for a bath. He always did that—just dumped things. But never mind that, now. Two watches in their presentation boxes. I mean . . . I had to peep inside— couldn't resist it. It wasn't *my* birthday, but that was what he had in there. Well . . . I mean

. . . I couldn't help looking, now could I! I knew one of them had to be hers—there was a birthday card in there, too. Pretty, pretty. Not addressed. Oh no—he'd take it to her himself. And it wasn't any old cheap thing, that watch. A Rolex. Expensive. Very. There was that other watch in there, too. Quartz. The consolation prize, that was. For me, you could bet. I was the one needing the consolation.'

'And quite justifiable,' Amelia put in. 'I can understand exactly how you felt, Connie.'

Connie flicked her a smile. 'I'd have smashed it, if I could,' she went on. 'The Rolex . . . though it seemed a pity—such a lovely thing it was. But I had it out of its box and I squeezed it. Stupid, really. If the glass *had* broken, I'd have cut my thumb. But it was tough glass. It didn't break.'

'It wouldn't be glass, Connie,' I told her. 'Crystal, or something. Sapphire, I believe. Artificial sapphire, perhaps. Something tough and unscratchable, it would have to be.'

Connie grimaced. 'Whatever it was, it didn't break, and I squeezed it as hard as I could.'

I glanced at Amelia, who said, 'With your thumb, Connie?'

'Yes.'

'Then there's your answer, Richard,' Amelia said, a note of triumph in her voice. I simply smiled, and nodded to her.

'If he'd come down from the bathroom,' said Connie, 'just at that time, he'd have had both the watches—cases and all—thrown in his face. Or one of them, anyway.'

'Which one?' I asked.

'The Rolex, of course.'

'But you didn't?'

'No. I put them both back in his briefcase— and waited. And sure enough . . . didn't he give me the cheap one! Of course he did. And I could have killed him, there and then.'

'But you didn't,' I repeated.

I glanced at Amelia. She had two fingers pressed to her lips; her eyes were bright.

Connie said, 'I just walked out of the room. Sometimes, that's the only thing left to do. Said nothing. And sure enough, an hour later, just before he went out, mumbling about something important to do at his office, the liar, he asked me if I liked the paltry, cheap thing he'd bought for me. And I smiled. Yes . . . really, I did. *That* sent him off. Said something about going to his office again, and went off with his Rolex—for her. Damn the woman.'

'So you understand, Connie,' I said, 'why I need to see him.'

CHAPTER FIVE

Eventually, and once convinced that there could be no danger of my actions involving her, or of any information that Harry felt prepared to reveal embarrassing her, Connie told me where I might locate him. As she had already told me, he had an office at Wolverhampton, as well as his office in Bridgnorth, and he was living in a flat just out of Wolverhampton, on the Shropshire side.

Though she had been to visit to him, Connie could not remember the exact address. Harry was living with a woman named Jean Clarke, whom she had already mentioned as being nervous of meeting Connie in person— she had hidden behind a chair, as Connie had put it. Whether or not she and Harry were married, Connie didn't know. She simply did not care, and, from what I was beginning to learn about Harry, it hardly seemed likely. My assessment of Harry, and that all from hearsay, did not credit him with any sense of responsibility, and I could confidently guess that he would not tie himself legally to any woman. All he wanted was that she should be willing to supply him with home comforts without the more usual and restrictive contract of marriage. As poor Sylvia Thomas had been.

We said goodbye to Connie, and I had to

admit that I didn't know when we would see her again.

My first instinct was to get back into Amelia's car, and go hunting out the address of Jean Clarke, but Amelia reminded me that it was nearly one o'clock, and Mary would have a meal ready for us, and would be distressed if we didn't turn up. So that was what we did, we went home, and the dogs, when we arrived, were clearly ready for their lunches, as well.

Afterwards, and with very little information to go on, I decided that we ought to try to find Harry, which, in practice, meant locating the flat belonging to Jean Clarke. There was such a person listed in the phone book, but the location was strange to me. Tettenhall. My map informed me that it was a suburb on the Shropshire side of Wolverhampton. I didn't know what to expect, nor how to find it, nor, indeed, whether this was Harry's Jean Clarke.

Consequently, I drove into Wolverhampton (which, I discovered later, I need not have done) with my eyes focused well ahead, hoping to find a police car, and extract information. Which I did. The two officers were parked beside the pavement, and were taking a break. They were only too eager to help. Perhaps they were bored. I was now heading in roughly the correct direction, they told me. And be careful at the road junction ahead, I was advised. I would see it signposted. They even knew the location of the block of flats where, I was hoping, I would find Jean Clarke.

'Up the hill,' the driver said. 'It's called The Rock, and keep your eyes open for a clock in a square tower, at the top and on the left. Turn left there, and past the shops, and you can't miss the block of flats, also on your left.'

'And oh,' the woman driver called after me, 'there's a car-park right behind it.'

Thanking them, I continued with our search. The Rock was suitably named, because it turned out to be a quite steep hill, hacked out through a formidable sandstone outcrop. It reared high, each side near-vertical. And there, at the top of the hill, like a sentry on guard, was the clock in the square tower. It was not registering the correct time.

There, we took the left turn, and had no difficulty locating the flats. The building was fairly new, and had perhaps been built at the same time as the public carpark, behind it, was laid out. This was very convenient. There was no limit to the parking time, and no charge.

Flat 36, the information board in the entrance lobby informed me. We mounted the stairs to the third floor. Thirty-six. I pressed the door-bell button.

I had been a little surprised at the apparent lack of security. One would have expected an entryphone in the lobby, at least, to check whether you were welcome, and a request to state your name and business, before even the flat number would be revealed. But no. There I was, after we had walked up to the third floor, listening to the echo of the door chimes, far down another hall, it seemed, and idly peering through a side window, the view from which at least must have given the residents a limited feeling of security. On the opposite side of the car-park entrance there was a police sub-station.

At my shoulder, the door having opened silently, a voice asked, 'What do you want?' It was a woman's voice, a hint of panic in it. 'Whatever you're selling, I don't want any.' She was a woman who recognised her own weaknesses.

'I don't blame you,' I said. It at least halted the movement of the closing door. 'All I want is confirmation that Harry Martin is living here, and information about when he's likely to be home.'

She was a very solid-looking lady, in her late thirties, perhaps, and with a heavy frown, which, if not conquered, was destined shortly to put years on her appearance. She made no move to open the door further, but she also gave no indication that she was about to slam it in my face.

'He lives here, yes,' she conceded. 'When he decides to put in an appearance, that is.'

'That must be awkward for you, then,' I said, smiling my sympathy. 'If he doesn't get round to you when the rent's due.'

This complete lack of good taste earned me a dig in the ribs from Amelia.

There was a long pause. Jean frowned, but it was a frown of concentration. Then she said, 'Oh—I see. You've got the wrong idea entirely. He bought this flat for me, outright. It's in my name. You obviously don't know him. He's very generous.'

'Oh . . .' I said, stalling for time. 'I didn't know he could afford—'

She cut me off with a small bark of laughter. 'Oh . . . you *obviously* don't know him. He works at advising and suggesting and helping, which I don't really understand—and he gets comm-something . . .'

'Commissions?'

'Yes. That's the word. And he must make quite a lot of money out of it—buying this flat outright, and I've got my own banking account . . .' She was clearly very proud of him.

Then she stopped, apparently suddenly aware that she was speaking of personal matters to strangers.

I said lightly, 'I must have been misled by that old Land Rover he uses.'

'Yes,' she comforted. 'You've got quite the wrong idea. He earns . . . oh, a lot of money—or so I believe.'

This information did not fit in with the old Land Rover, but perhaps it was convenient, if he travelled a large number of pot-holed back lanes in order to discover old and careworn stately homes, of possible interest to his clients.

'But he's not here now?' I probed.

She shook her head vigorously, pursing her lips. 'Haven't seen him since yesterday. There was a phone call for him. Last night. Ten-ish. But do come inside.'

It didn't sound hopeful. I was beginning to realise that Harry, apparently being a go-between in financial matters relating to property sales, could be anywhere at any time, seeming to have various *pieds-à-terre* with sundry women, who were willing, and perhaps anxious, to find a bed for him for a night. Harry was emerging as a wandering Casanova.

'Any idea where he could be?' I asked, not with any optimism.

'Not too precisely,' she admitted. 'Do you know Beaudesert Park?'

'Well . . . no. Never heard of it.'

'It's the other side of Cannock. Beaudesert Park in Cannock Chase. All woodland and tracks and the like. He said he was going to advise a client on the purchase of a house in this Beaudesert Park. I don't expect it's the Manor House, of course. Oh no. But in the Park, which is the important thing. It's one of those select locations that the wealthy people look for. Mary Queen of Scots was imprisoned there, or so I'm told. In the Manor House, I'd expect.'

She seemed, once she'd started talking, as

94

though she would never stop. I cut in quickly.

'And it's there I might hope to find him?'

I was feeling very doubtful about all this. Of course, it was not Harry's wealth—or lack of it—that I needed to consider. He would be there to advise a client: how easy or difficult it might be for the client to raise the money. For the Manor House, which, I could guess, would have the doubtful lure of the possible ghost of Mary Queen of Scots, they would be talking in figures so remote from what my bank manager recommended as a basic deposit necessary to continue my daily existence, that I might, at best, acquire one of their stables and install a truckle bed. It was just as well that my yearnings never wandered into that sphere of existence. I couldn't help wondering, therefore, who Harry's potential client might be.

I had no specific feelings of aversion towards Harry. Contempt, yes, but I left any antipathy in Connie's safe control. Nevertheless, I had a feeling that he was walking a none-too-steady tightrope, and one that was frayed near to breaking, into the bargain. But as far as I knew, his actions were doing nobody any harm, so that he was free to continue his vague wanderings from woman to woman, though there was always the chance that somebody would eventually put a stop to his sexual activities.

Ten-ish, she had said. It was a strange time

for him to have left on a business trip, late the previous evening. Surely he could not have arranged to meet a client at night, in Beaudesert Park, which didn't sound as though it would be brightly lit with street lamps. There were probably no streets, let alone lamps.

There was no chance of seeing him at the flat, I decided. We therefore made our apologies to Jean Clarke, for wasting her time, and said we ought to be on our way.

'Oh . . . really? Must you?' She was clearly feeling lonely without Harry, and craved company. She was exactly the type of woman who would become a prey to him.

'I'm afraid so,' said Amelia. 'Do you hear that howling sound?' She waited for Jean's nod. 'That's our dogs, getting bored with waiting.'

'You could let them wait, bored or not. I'm bored, most of the time,' she admitted.

I shook my head. Amelia said, looking round at the view from the window, 'Isn't that a patch of grass I can see? The far side of the shops.'

'Yes. The Green, it's called. It's the other side of the main road. There's a paddling pool there, so-called, but it's too cold for paddling at the beginning of November. They'll have drained it, I expect. There's a parking place as well. Harry parks his Land Rover there, or so I understand.'

'Shall we go and have a look at it, then?' I

asked Amelia. 'Give the dogs a run.'

'Yes. We'll do that.'

Then, by exhibiting a strong yearning to view this area of grassland and the pool, even though dry, we managed to ease our way out of the door. Jean Clarke was obviously not going to be able to offer any more help.

The collecting of the dogs was a little difficult. Having been left in charge of the car—as they would see it—they were full of boisterous and pent-up energy, and nearly had me over. Go for the leads first, that was the technique. Then, having secured them, I felt more relaxed. It didn't always work out right, and more than once I'd had to chase them and whistle them in. This time, it was just a matter of holding on grimly to the leads. Leaving the car where it was, we began to walk in the general direction of the paddling pool, me leaning well back.

I wasn't sure what to make of the shopping centre. Certainly it was too extensive to claim that this was a village, and not large enough to justify the title of a township. A branch of one of the banks, two building society sub-offices, and the usual shops, even a small arcade; all these were present.

We negotiated a large area of grassland, with huge trees around us, so placidly solid that they must have been there long before the foundations for the first of the shops had been excavated. It was not dog-running territory, as busy streets seemed to surround us. And then—a road to cross, a main road, heading out of these suburbs into the leafy lanes of Shropshire, and carrying a steady flow of traffic. Fortunately, there were traffic lights at a pedestrian crossing. Already the dogs were lifting their heads, aware of a possible good run ahead.

Once we were on the other side, and walking on grass again, we could afford to look around. Lush, green grass ran away into the distance, but the paddling pool was quite close. We had it all to ourselves, I saw, apart from one old man, placidly smoking a black and ancient meerschaum pipe, and with one leg up on a bench seat which he had commandeered, and which overlooked the drained pool. He was well wrapped up, was probably there all day, every day, summer and winter. Nothing else to do.

'Nice day,' he said. 'You can let 'em off their leads, you know. They won't trouble me.'

It could, indeed, be described as a nice day, for early November. But he would surely be cold, sitting there. I nevertheless unclipped the dogs' leads.

They went directly to him to check that he was friendly, decided he was, and then focused their expectations on the paddling pool. Well . . . it had the general appearance of a paddling pool, a kind of kidney shape with crimps in it, and though it had been drained, there had been rain since then. And wind. And fallen leaves—even branches—from the magnificent trees all around it. The result was that the soggy brown leaves were deep at the one end of the dry pool, where the wind had piled them up, though the rest of the pool was clear, down to the concrete surface.

Undeterred by the not-very-pleasant brown mush of leaves, the dogs plunged in, woofing away with excitement.

Amelia said, 'The car's going to smell terrible by the time we get home.'

Sheba and Jake were happily digging their way into this noxious leaf pile. Now I was regretting the fact that I had let them run loose. Amelia had been quite correct; the dogs were freeing a terrible smell. But there was no reason for them to be quite so excited about it, I thought. I tried calling them in, but they did no more than increase the volume of their barks, no more than glance back at us, welcoming us to go and share this marvellous and odious discovery.

I then realised that the discovery included more than leaves. What abruptly shot free from the leaf pile was a shoe. A man's shoe. This seemed to drive the dogs crazy; they rushed towards us, barking now more urgently, forward and back. Look, look, what we've found! And the shoe, tossed free of the leaf pile, revealed a sock—and then another shoe, which they frantically pulled at, until the whole heaped pile of leaves quivered, and I realised what it was that they had found.

Almost falling on my face, I jumped down the eighteen inches to the concrete base. My first task was to get a firm grip on the leads. This was not difficult, as Sheba and Jake were now involved, with enthusiasm, in their efforts to wrap the leads around my legs. Managing to untangle them, one at a time, I got a good grip on each lead, and with my arms nearly being pulled out of their sockets, struggled back to the edge of the pool. The old chap from the bench was now standing beside Amelia.

'Tie 'em to the bench,' he suggested.

But no—the two of them together were powerful enough to pull the bench over and drag it along. I took a firm grip on their leads and said quietly to Amelia, 'Do you remember the police sub-station, love?'

'Yes. Of course. By the car-park.'

'Then will you go there and tell whoever's on duty—probably only one constable—that there's apparently a human body lying under that pile of leaves. If there's nobody there, you'll probably find a phone in the lobby. No need to dial. Pick it up, and you'll be connected to the central station in town. Tell them . . . but you know what to say. A dead man under the leaves. Tell them we'll wait here.'

'Yes, Richard.' Amelia pursed her lips, her eyes gleaming. She knew exactly what to do and what to say. 'And I'll come straight back to here?'

'Yes, love.'

'And you're sure there's a dead man under there?'

'Absolutely certain. Look at the dogs—they're frantic. There's more than just a pair of shoes under those leaves. And I'd risk a good bet that I know whose shoes they are, too.'

'Harry's?' she whispered.

I nodded. 'Harry,' I agreed. 'You could almost say he had it coming to him. But don't say anything about identity to the police. It'd only lead to a long and complicated explanation, and it might not be Harry, after all. It's only a hunch. I'll wait here and guard the location, and tell them what they need to know.'

She grimaced, turned away, and headed back to the crossing with the traffic lights. This, of course, promoted a surge of energy from both of the dogs. They didn't like Amelia to be separated from me. Well . . . neither did I.

'It's all right,' I said, quite quietly, and they looked up at me, panting, and searching for more fun.

I recalled what Connie had said about having Harry put down.

'Can't see how he got there,' said the old man, suddenly at my elbow.

'Perhaps he fell in. If it was night. Ten

101

o'clock, say. Dark around here, I'd guess.'

'Not all that dark.'

He knew this place, had probably lived in the same house since childhood, when he himself had paddled in this pool. I looked around. There were street lights, which I knew would be orange when lit, these not very far away, along the main road. And, I saw, there was a side road, which flanked the grassland and the pool, this too with its own lights, though rather scattered. But at night, nobody would have reason for being in the vicinity of the pool. It would not provide anything resembling a short-cut from the road to anywhere else. But . . . I looked around me, more attentive than before. Beyond a scattering of trees and a fair amount of hedges, were visible the roofs of a number of cars. Well yes, I thought. In the summer, this small portion of parkland, with its pool, would attract many families, who would need somewhere to park their cars without having to cross a busy main road on foot. And there it was, its entrance obviously from the side street. They were well served with parking surfaces around there, I thought, and also the necessary facilities, as I could just detect, in a far corner, what looked like a double set of public toilets. After all, the paddling pool would help in attracting customers to the shops.

Then, even as I watched, a police car, blue

beacon flashing but with no siren operating, turned off from the main road, and drove past us into the car-park, at which I was at that moment staring. A small van followed it. Quietly, they came. No need to make a fuss about it. No need to alarm the people who were spending their money in this small township, as I'd decided to call it in my mind. There was money in this district. They would expect consideration from their guardians of the law. And this was what they got. The two police vehicles drove into the car-park provided, quietly and without fuss. Three men and a woman, all in uniform, alighted, and walked towards us—one sergeant and three constables. Amelia was once again, and suddenly, at my side.

'What's this about a dead person?' asked the sergeant, who was the woman. 'There's been mention of a man's shoe.'

I could detect the fact that she hadn't seriously accepted the details, as they would have been radio-ed to her. A dead person, seemingly male, in the paddling pool, as the shoe pulled off by the dogs was apparently a man's. This much, she would have been told. Yet no corpse was to be seen.

'Whatever sex it is,' I told her, 'it was wearing men's shoes.' I held up the rescued shoe for her to view the evidence. 'The dogs . . .' They now sat relaxed and placidly, one each side of me, panting. '. . . they must have detected something. Can't have been a human smell, I'd have thought. Those rotting leaves would've drowned out any other smell. In any event, however they detected whatever it is, *they* dug into the pile and found a shoe. This shoe. Then a sock and another shoe. And at that stage I dragged them away.'

'So we can't be certain it's a man,' she said, nodding her understanding.

'It's a man's shoe.'

'That doesn't have to mean that there's a body of a man to go with it. The shoes could just have been discarded.'

'Want a bet?' I asked flatly. The woman was beginning to annoy me. She was thinking all round the situation, but not in respect of her next action. Rather, on the lines of how she might, so easily in this situation, make a fool of herself by shouting out for assistance, when there was only a pair of shoes that had been retrieved by Sheba and Jake. I could not blame her. Maybe she was working under a chauvinistic inspector, whom she hated. I changed my attitude, no longer annoyed by her lack of decisiveness, merely suggesting a bet.

'I don't gamble,' she told me. 'Just doing this job is enough of a gamble for me.'

'All right,' I said quietly, my eyes on the young male constable, about ten yards away, who had driven their car there, and who was now staring ahead and pretending not to hear a word. 'The facts,' I went on. 'That pile of leaves seems to have been blown there in the past day or two. All the trees are shedding their leaves. If the wind whipped along this pool last night—'

'It did,' said the old man at my elbow, determined to remain in touch. 'Me . . . I dropped off, sort of. A bit of a nap. It was the cold wind that woke me up.'

'Then you were lucky,' said the woman sergeant sharply. 'It's so blasted easy. You doze off, and the temperature drops, and damn it all, you might not wake up again. Don't you know that?' She eyed him up and down, with severe disapproval.

The old chap looked surprised at her firmness. 'It isn't much warmer at my place, I can tell y' that,' he grumbled.

'And where's that?' she demanded. Then she raised her voice. 'Merridew, let's have you here for a minute.'

The constable seemed to jerk out of a trance. He had been staring at the leaf pile, leaning over the lip of the pool as far as he dared. He came, but not as quickly as he might have done, had his sergeant been a man.

'Take a note of this,' she told him. 'Now, sir,' she continued with the old man. 'I take it that you live around here?'

'Yus,' he said, a reluctance creeping in to blur the word.

'Address, then?' she asked him.

Sullenly, staring at his feet, he gave his

address.

'That's the old court, isn't it?' she asked. 'Round the back of the fire station?'

'Yus.'

'I thought so. What number?'

He shrugged. 'Haven't got any numbers. I call my place Nirvana.'

'Do you?' Her eyebrows shot up.

'Gotta call it something, haven't I? No numbers, see.'

'I suppose so. Now, if you'll just go back to your bench—if you haven't got anything better to do—you can sit and watch what happens. Then, when it's been sorted out, we'll go for a cup of tea. All right?' She smiled as the old chap stared at her. 'And a currant bun,' she added.

He nodded. I thought for a moment that he was going to salute. His hand was shaping up for it.

'But first,' she asked him, 'just tell me . . . how long has that heap of leaves been there?'

'Wasn't that big when I went home last night. Well . . . mounting up, it was. Wind came whistlin' along here. Sharp wind. You could hear the rustling. The leaves,' he added, to make sure she understood.

'But not see it?' she asked. 'Not watch it building up?'

He shook his head. 'Told you, didn't I! Dozed off a bit. And *anyway*, the street lights aren't so bright.'

'All right. Thank you. Now . . . you go and sit in the car. It'll be warmer.'

He was reluctant, but he did as she wished, ambling along with his shoulders slumped.

'Now,' she said, turning to the constable. 'What've we got that'll shift those leaves? Something not too hefty.'

'There's that bit of a rake we picked up, Shipley way.'

'Ideal. Fetch it along, then, and let's do a bit of leaf clearing. But gently, Merridew. We don't know what might be under there.'

But I did. Oh yes, I knew.

Then we watched as Merridew got down to it and, inside five minutes, Merridew being very careful indeed, and discovering that his hands were more effective than the rake, there was revealed again the other shoe, but this one was where it ought to have been—on a foot. Then a leg . . . then the other leg, and there was no longer any reason to dispute the fact that what the leaves had been covering was the body of a man.

The sergeant said quietly to me, 'You expected this, didn't you?'

She now seemed to be taking me seriously, conceding that I might know what I was talking about.

'I expected something like this, anyway,' I told her. 'Violence in one aspect or another. Harry Martin, I'm guessing at—and it was ten years ago that I had dealings with him. He was a womaniser. Lady friends all over the place. But—give him his due—they were, and probably have always been, either single or widows, mostly. Otherwise, I'd say, he'd have been killed a lot earlier. But certainly, he's probably ruined quite a number of relationships, in his time. Really, he had it coming to him.'

'How come you know him so well?' she asked, not pushing it, making her question sound casual.

'Another violent death,' I told her. 'Over Bridgnorth way, in a house overlooking the Severn. At the time, it seemed to be a quite obvious case. The dead woman had been one of Harry Martin's lady friends, so naturally I looked round, and concentrated on his legal partner, the wife. And the evidence led to her trial for the murder of that mistress. She was found guilty, and she's recently been released from prison. But now . . . there's doubt as to her guilt, so I'm looking around again, hoping for new evidence. And of course, he's still been at it. That's why I say that Harry Martin had it coming to him. In fact, I'd have expected to hear that at least he'd been beaten up. But I haven't heard anything of that.'

'There's more than that,' she suggested. 'Sure to be.'

'Yes,' I agreed. 'Much more. In any event, I wanted to meet him again. We met, of course, at the time of that woman's death. There was no suggestion at all that he might have killed her. There'd have been no motive. But . . . I've traced him to here. One of his current lady friends lives in that block of flats, next to the other parking area.' I pointed in the general direction, and she nodded. 'Opposite your sub-station. Her name's Jean Clarke. She told me he'd left her flat at around ten o'clock yesterday evening. There was a phone call for him. I'd wanted a word or two with him, and now I'll never know.'

She was showing signs of impatience. Obviously, she had hoped to extract something vitally important as to the background of this death.

'Never know what?' she demanded, quite briskly now.

'In relationship to that other murder—ten years ago—where he was on that evening, whether it was anywhere near the site of Sylvia Thomas's death. That was the woman's name.'

'Hmm!' she said, as we had wandered into uncharted areas, as far as she was concerned.

'May I suggest,' I asked her, 'that you tell the constable to leave that pile of leaves alone? If I were you I'd get on to my central station and report to my senior officer. He'll surely want to get the scenes of crime team on it.'

'You think it's not . . .' She paused, considering how best to say it.

'Not an accident?' I asked. 'I'm certain it

wasn't. And I can make a fair guess that it's Harry Martin. Now I'm too late—I've lost him. Quite frankly, from what I know about the man, I'm surprised that somebody hasn't done it earlier.'

She shot me a sharp, inquisitive glance. 'You're ex-police, aren't you?'

'That's so. An ex-DI. What say that I stand here and guard the site, while you get on your car radio to your super? Tell him it doesn't look like an accident. And for heaven's sake, don't disturb that leaf pile any more—not one leaf.'

She grimaced, perhaps intending it as a smile. Then she turned away, and went back to her car, having called off the leaf-clearing constable.

The old chap, suddenly at my shoulder, said, 'There goes that cup of tea she promised. And the bun.'

'I wouldn't be so sure of that, my friend,' I told him. 'But it won't be in any café around here.'

'Where, then?' He was very suspicious.

'Along at the station.' I felt Amelia jerk at my jacket. She thought I was teasing him. I told him, 'They'll need you. You'll be their chief witness.' To boost his morale.

'I haven't witnessed anything.' He was obviously much concerned.

'They'll look after you,' I promised on their behalf. 'You're very valuable to them. How's that make you feel?'

But his eyes were searching around for an escape route. 'Damn rotten,' he told me. 'I ain't never been in no copper shop, not never.'

This translated as a statement that he had never been inside a police station, and didn't want to become involved—and make it a habit.

But I had a feeling that he was exaggerating his grammar on purpose. His idea of light relief, perhaps.

'Why can't they leave me alone?' he complained. 'Why can't they leave me alone?'

'You're important, that's why.' I had to go on with it, trying to reassure him, but Amelia's tugs at my sleeve were becoming more urgent. 'They're not going to chuck you into a cell, not going to shout at you, not going to do anything but thank you for helping them,' I told him.

'How can I help 'em?' he demanded. 'All I've bloody well done is sit on that flamin' bench, and *that* wasn't all that comfortable, I can tell you.'

'So,' I said, 'if that seat wasn't very comfortable, you wouldn't have sat there too late—you'd have gone home. What time *did* you go home?'

'Dunno.'

'You must—'

'Got no watch, have I?'

'There's a clock facing you, the other side of the road,' I pointed out. This was the one for which the police constable at Wolverhampton had told me to look.

'Hah!' he said. 'A lot of use, that is. It's stopped. It's more stopped than going.'

'And you can't even guess?' I urged him.

He shrugged. 'Ten-ish, I suppose. Around that.'

'And you saw nobody walking by the pool?'

'Nah!'

'That dead man—he would've been walking in that direction.'

'Told y', didn't I! I saw nowt.'

There had been no reference to a wife, waiting for him to come home, nor of a cat or dog that needed feeding. It seemed to me that he was independent, living completely alone on his old-age pension.

'Takin' their time about it, aren't they?' he asked.

'They always do.' Which wasn't strictly true. But in fact, a van had just drawn into the parking lot behind us, and another police car followed it. The big guns were being brought into action. The technicians were about to dissect every smallest leaf in that pile, and minutely inspect every square inch of the pool's concrete surface, and that before they paid much attention to the body itself. The woman sergeant walked away briskly, in order to intercept her senior officer.

CHAPTER SIX

The old man, I knew, was shortly going to become a very important person to the local police. He might protest that he had seen nothing, but my experience reminded me that a witness's version of nothing could often turn out to become a very important something to an investigating officer. It needed only a little encouragement.

The uniformed police sergeant was now approaching us again. I sensed the old chap stiffening beside me.

'Am you comin' along wi' we?' she asked him, lapsing into Black Country slang, which she obviously thought would relax him.

But he had no choice in the matter. 'Got no bloody choice, have I?' he said, having realised it.

'You're our main witness,' she told him, playing gently on his ego. 'Can't risk losing you. Now come along, into my car. I'll run you home, afterwards.' And strangely, she winked at me.

Then I understood. Unusual in a police officer, who is trained to be impartial, she had become interested in the old man's situation. Run him home afterwards? I knew that trick. He would almost be forced into inviting her into his domain, from a basic instinct of politeness. And she was about to commit what is almost a sin, to a police officer. That was to become personally involved. I recalled, then, her concern over his drifting into sleep on that cold bench. Oh dear, I thought. His quiet and uneventful existence was shortly to be disrupted. She would bring down on him teams of social workers, home helps, and district nurses, protest as he might; and whether or not he approved, he would be monitored. He had abruptly become an important person, the only one who could have been within sight of the murder. But—give the officer her due credit—I could see that she was to become his guardian, making sure that he received all he was entitled to from the social services, and undermining his independence, whether he liked it or not.

I said, 'If it's any use to you, I can tell your senior officer that I think I know the identity of the person you people are about to uncover.'

'Ah . . . yes?' She shot me a glance of doubt. Then, cocking her head, 'Perhaps you'd better have a word with him.' And she looked round in search of him.

Amelia said quietly, 'Richard, we can't afford to get involved with this.' She tugged at my sleeve, as emphasis.

I agreed. The dogs were restless; there were large stretches of grass within reach, and they were being expected to sit quietly, when all they wanted to do was chase around like mad things.

'I'm afraid we're already involved, love,' I told her. 'Certainly, I am.'

'We'll be stuck here . . .'

'I'll keep it short.' I tried to sound optimistic.

- 'Hah!' she said. 'Can you imagine the situation if they start questioning you? As they will, as soon as they realise that you know something about this. You'll be stuck here,' she repeated. 'Hours, perhaps. How can you expect me to drive home, with the dogs, and leave you behind? They'd go berserk.'

'But we can't just walk away from it.'

'Can't we?' she demanded. 'Just watch my heels. I can do it.'

'Now . . . Amelia . . .'

We were about to plunge into our first serious disagreement. If we went our separate ways, if only temporarily, as Amelia had said, the dogs would go wild.

And approaching me, from one of the recently parked cars, was a hefty man in a tight-fitting brown suit, who didn't look as though he would stand for any procrastination. He had had a few quick words with the uniformed sergeant who had been first on the scene, and he was now walking towards us with steady and purposeful strides, his objective clearly me.

'I understand you can tell us something

about this,' he said. 'Superintendent Fisher,' he introduced himself.

'Richard Patton,' I offered. 'Ex-DI. I'm here, in this district, because I've been trying to trace a man named Harry Martin, on behalf of his ex-wife. They're divorced. Things I wanted to ask him. This is a guess, of course, but I did get as far as to find out that he's been staying with a woman named Jean Clarke, near here. Temporarily,' I added. 'He never seemed to stay anywhere very long. From what I've been discovering, he could very well have had a number of lady friends in this region, all of them willing to accommodate him. If there's a battered old Land Rover parked over there . . .' I gestured towards the car-park behind us. 'That would be his. It seems that he used it in his work. He was an adviser on money matters involving property sales. And that's about all I can tell you. He was obviously the kind of person who does get done in, eventually. An entrepreneur, that's the word. He took on the wives when the husbands were temporarily absent.'

'Hmm!' He was dubious. 'But you're guessing.'

'That's true. There's just a chance that it isn't Harry Martin.'

He looked round at the activities behind him. 'Will you come and have a proper look at him?' he asked.

I shrugged. 'It's been ten years since I've

seen Harry Martin—and that was to do with another murder. Not on your patch—over Bridgnorth way. But I'll look and see whether I can remember him.'

He was dubious. 'You mentioned another murder. What other murder?'

I said nothing. Just shook my head. No point in introducing side issues.

But he wasn't intending to leave it at that. 'If there's been another murder, I need to know.'

I glanced at Amelia, who frowned at me. She knew I couldn't leave it there. 'Ten years ago,' I told him, 'a woman was killed, in her own house, and she was one of Harry's woman friends. His wife went on trial for that murder, was found guilty, and has been released only very recently. But Harry Martin's habits don't seem to have changed. I'm afraid not all his lovers were single, and I'd expect that when the news of his death gets in the papers, there could be a certain number of husbands who won't be doing any grieving.'

'You haven't looked at him yet,' he reminded me, a little sourly. He wasn't going to waste any mental energy in guessing what the outcome of Harry's death might be.

'No. True. I haven't,' I agreed.

So I went across to where they were picking off the last of the leaves from the body. He had fallen in a position facing upwards. But nevertheless I could not make a decision with confidence. I looked round at Fisher.

'I can't be certain. Ten years . . .' And the man's features were distorted by a split-second reaction to the blow. 'I think you'll have to rely on what's in his pockets.'

Fisher grunted. 'All right. If it's like that.'

'I'm afraid it is.'

That was a pity. It meant that the superintendent now had to involve Jean Clarke in this distasteful business, and possibly, later on, Connie.

It seemed to be a somewhat macabre coincidence that Harry Martin, in exactly the same way as Sylvia Thomas, had died from a hefty blow on the head with a chunk of wood, or something else like that, and as heavy. The police were still searching the area for such a weapon, and several branches, stripped from the trees by the recent high winds, appeared to fit the bill. But to my mind, though I do not pretend to have anything but a minimum knowledge of forensic science, it seemed that the actual contusion, when I managed to snatch a quick glance, was rather narrow for any of the heavier branches that lay around the paddling pool. Any that were sufficiently slim would probably have been too light and flimsy.

I turned away, and left them to it.

CHAPTER SEVEN

One of the difficulties with which we now had to cope was that Detective Superintendent Fisher wished to interview both Amelia and myself, as he had realised that we might know quite a lot about the background to Harry's death. With four of us, which included Fisher's woman sergeant, and also the two dogs, the only suitable accommodation, and that not really adequate, was the police van. The seating was cramped, precedence having been given to the fact that it was an operational laboratory, as close as I can describe it. We didn't have them in my days. But now we managed to find seating for the four of us, with the dogs sprawled at our feet, and grumbling in their throats whenever Fisher's voice took on an authoritative tone.

'Can't you go and tie these damned dogs outside?' he demanded.

'No,' I said, and left it at that.

He didn't seem pleased. 'Hmm! All right. Let's get on with it, then. You believe that the dead man is someone called Harry Martin. You'll be pleased to hear that the contents of his pockets confirm that. The address on his driving licence is in Bridgnorth.'

'Yes,' I agreed. 'That could be so. He's got an office—'

'We know,' he cut in. 'The address is a flat on the floor above.'

'That sounds logical.' I nodded. 'I think you'll find he's got a similar set-up in Wolverhampton. Difficult to locate him, unless you had an appointment. That would be typical of him.'

'What you'd call a wanderer,' Fisher said gloomily, because it was beginning to seem that other police forces in other districts were going to be involved. 'Wife?' he asked. 'Is there a wife?'

'They're divorced. That seems to have come about because of the murder I mentioned. Nine years his wife—ex-wife, now—has served in prison. She's out now, but certainly not anxious to become involved with him in any way.'

'So at least,' said Fisher sourly, 'there'll be somebody who'll be relieved to hear he's dead.'

'But not his ex-wife. She erased him from her mental list of acquaintances a long while ago.'

'Hmm!' he said. 'Any other contacts?' He was still a little uncertain about identification.

'Dozens of female contacts, I'd guess,' I told him.

'Any around here—in this district?' Fisher managed to look a little more optimistic.

'I think I've already mentioned Jean Clarke,' I said. 'She's the last one to have seen him alive. That was when he left her flat yesterday evening. Ten o'clock-ish.'

He grunted. 'The last one apart from his murderer. Or perhaps she could have followed him, this Jean Clarke?'

He left that as a question, as he saw that I was not keen on it.

'I don't think so.' I glanced at Amelia. She shook her head. 'You'll no doubt want to see her—question her. But I'm sure you'll agree, if you see her . . . she's not the violent type.'

'Hmm!' He wasn't impressed. 'My experience with women is that they can be very violent indeed.'

Amelia, who hadn't said a word for ages, reacted to this remark. 'I could dispute that,' she said. 'Even if pushed, most women wouldn't resort to violence. Not *this* sort of violence.'

'Hmm!' said the superintendent. 'We'd better not get involved with *that* proposition. Some of the things I've witnessed . . . well, never mind that. But I'll see this Jean Clarke, and I'm afraid, Mr Patton, that she'll have to confirm—or not—your identification.'

'Yes,' I agreed. 'It'd be as well.'

'So . . . assuming he *is* Harry Martin, now deceased, I'll have to ask you what you know about him.'

'All right,' I agreed again. I looked around me. 'I assume you've got a tape-recorder somewhere in here, busily recording every word.'

He looked blank. Which meant that he had.

I grinned at him, then told him what he needed to know. 'Harry Martin . . . his basic characteristic would have to be his sexual proclivities. Every contact I've made with people who know about him . . . the information has been the same. He was over-sexed. And, assuming some of his women had husbands—or regular gentlemen friends—then he was living rather dangerously. I don't say that's the only motivation for his death. Just a starter. But it does mean you'll need to trace these men—husbands and men friends of the women Harry Martin knew so intimately. So I don't envy you, because it'll mean contacting them by way of the women friends, which means—'

'Never mind,' he cut in, raising a palm to silence me. 'I know what's to be done. With a bit of luck, he might even have a notebook somewhere, full of names and addresses of these women . . .'

'And you'll trace every one of the men from their wives or sweethearts? Oh dear me. I don't envy you, Superintendent. I don't. But . . . if you like, I'll start it all off by visiting Jean Clarke. I can perhaps smooth your way. You're going to have to ask her to view the body—at the morgue—and I could help her through that ordeal.'

The superintendent grimaced. 'Thank you,

Mr Patton, but I think not. I'll need to observe her reaction to Martin's death—if it is him.'

'Oh . . . it's him. You'll find it is. You don't want me to break the news to her, then?'

'Thank you . . . no. Just tell me her address and flat number.'

Which I did. For a second I contemplated getting to Jean Clarke first, whether he liked it or not. I was certain I could break the news more gently than this Superintendent Fisher. But . . . looking back to her attitude when we had been talking about Harry, I couldn't imagine her collapsing into a faint, however clumsy Fisher might be.

So . . . names and address taken from us, and with the comment that he might need to come and visit us later, he allowed us to go on our way, and was good enough to tell us that there was a convenient short-cut we could take in order to get on the Wolverhampton to Bridgnorth Road.

'Bridgnorth would be about fifteen miles from here,' he said. Twenty minutes' run to our home, I realised. Which gave me a spare few minutes in which to reconstruct in my mind the death of Harry Martin. Standing on the rim of the paddling pool, I tried to activate my imagination.

I could envision him crossing from the other side of the road by way of the traffic lights, then heading past the pool to the small car-park behind us, and to his Land Rover.

Someone had phoned for a rendezvous. Not much traffic. But the street lights would have been on, though the wind in the trees would have tossed the branches around, throwing shadows before him, and making it difficult to place his feet accurately. Was that what had happened? Something as prosaic as missing his footing and falling, in such a manner that he'd struck his head against the rounded rim of the paddling pool, and died in that way? But no. The police had seemed certain that he'd suffered a heavy blow to the crown of his head, as it seemed to me, and equally certain that they had managed to find a loose branch that matched with the contusion. In any event, the blow had been to the crown, which would not have been the case if he'd done no more than fall.

No . . . the scenario had to include an assailant, someone who had watched Harry's movements, had waited, had intended to kill him, and had done so, and, indeed, could well have been the one to phone him. More than likely.

It was time, Amelia thought, that we should be heading home. 'We ought to be phoning Mary. You know she worries terribly if we're away too long. I noticed a phone booth across the road,' she added.

'All right.'

We crossed together, if only to satisfy the dogs, and I stood there as Amelia phoned. In about a minute she joined us again.

'Mary's worried that you'll have to drive home in the dark,' she said. Mary always feared night driving.

'It's not dark,' I pointed out.

I rather wished that it was. I would have liked to see just what the visibility around the paddling pool would be, with the shop windows dark and shuttered, and the street lamps lit. But Amelia had promised that we would be on our way in a minute or two. Call it a quarter of an hour. 'Just a minor detail I want to clear up,' I explained.

So off we went again, across the street at the traffic lights, around the paddling pool, and there was the old chap, still sprawled on his bench.

'Did you get your cup of tea and the currant bun?' I asked him.

He shook his head. 'Not yet. Said she'd be back, got to sign off, or somethin'. And it isn't going to be tea and a bun. A proper cooked dinner, she said, at the Premier Caff, round the corner.'

'Well . . . fine,' I congratulated him.

'So I've nipped back to my place and had a shave, and changed into my best suit.' He shot me a glance of embarrassment, but his smile indicated that he was, in some obscure way, leading me on.

'What next!' said Amelia, but quietly to me.

'Well . . . have a good time, friend,' I said. 'It

pays to keep in with the police.'

Then we walked on, heading for the small car-park and leaving him grinning, on what he probably thought of as *his* bench. I wondered again whether the grin indicated that he had been pulling my leg.

'Why have we come here?' Amelia asked.

I shrugged. 'It doesn't really matter. I just wanted to check that Harry Martin had a logical reason for walking in this direction. His Land Rover, in the car-park, there, seems to be the obvious answer, but why, if he'd been visiting Jean Clarke, wouldn't he have parked in *that* car-park? As we did.'

'Oh . . . Richard! That must be obvious. Jean Clarke wouldn't want her neighbours to see him parking that dirty old thing right under her window.'

'It's not that disreputable. Let's go and have a look at it.

Which we did. The hedgerow along this side of the car-park was not an unbroken run. Hedges . . . but spread in a haphazard way, suggesting the possibility that they had been, a vast number of years before, self-seeded. There was no difficulty in pushing through to the car-park's tarmac surface.

And there it was, Harry's Land Rover. Waiting for him—though he wouldn't be coming back. I walked round it, peering in, and being careful not to touch anything. But there was nothing to see that might have relevance to anything. I was wasting my time.

But perhaps not completely, because I noticed that he had left the ignition key in its lock, which was strange. There were quite a large number of keys on that ring, most of them of the cylinder lock type, so that I was looking at the collection he had needed for the numerous doors of his various lady friends, should they not be at home when he paid them a casual and unscheduled visit.

How many women would be shedding tears when the report of his death appeared in the local papers? Or perhaps . . . how many sighs of relief? I couldn't imagine that many might mourn. Connie, certainly not.

But . . . didn't the presence of the keys indicate that he had left them deliberately, having offered to lend the Land Rover for someone else's use? Then, later perhaps, he had realised that this was a foolish thing to do, and had been on his way to rectify that action. Yet I had to take into account the phone call to Jean Clarke's flat, and his departure at ten o'clock. Had this been a lure—perhaps completely unrelated to the keys?

But Amelia was tugging at my elbow. 'Aren't we leaving, Richard?' she asked. 'We ought to have left ages ago, really. You know how Mary worries.'

For a moment I had difficulty in dragging my mind from the question of the presence of the keys in the Land Rover, but with an effort

I shrugged the thought away. It seemed useless to play around with vague conjectures, particularly as I had to wipe my mind clear of the problem. I was going to be doing the driving.

I left the Land Rover's keys where they were. No doubt Superintendent Fisher would impound them, in due course, as part of Harry's estate. But . . . who would be Harry's heir? Not Connie . . . she was his ex-wife . . . Let the lawyers argue that one. It was time to go. I went back to where Amelia was waiting.

Mary had been quite correct with her reservations. Not only was the sun declining, but a black cloud was creeping up from the horizon, with the obvious intention of blanking off the sun.

We walked quite briskly back to our car-park and Amelia's car. The dogs appeared to have tired themselves out, because they at once stretched out on the rear seat, and settled down to a bit of a nap. So we were now free to leave.

The short-cut that Fisher had mentioned proved to lead exactly where he had said—to a traffic island. Bridgnorth . . . straight ahead. It was signposted. Within five minutes I seemed to have shaken off all the other traffic, because the road was almost deserted. Very shortly, though, there would be the steady stream of rush-hour traffic, all heading home, in both directions, from a hard day's work.

Once out on the open road, I found that the driving was straightforward. A speed limit of 50 mph was indicated, but I had no urge to travel faster. I was tired and worried, and had to force myself to concentrate.

Creeping back into the forefront of my mind, from time to time, was the disturbing puzzle of how Harry's key-ring had found its way to the dashboard of the Land Rover. I was finding it difficult to accept that Harry had been struck down simply in order to remove the bunch of keys from his pocket. It had been a vicious blow, far too forceful, if the keys had been the objective. And if this was so, why had the keys been left in the ignition lock? I was therefore forced to accept that he had left the keys in by mistake, and that the blow had been intended as a killing one, quite unrelated to the acquisition of the keys.

And where did that get me? Nowhere. There could be quite a number of people who would feel much more relaxed after hearing of Harry's death. But none who would have killed him simply for the keys, surely.

'Do keep your eyes on the road, Richard,' said Amelia.

Yes, I *had* taken that last bend rather too fast. Large and heavy spots of rain were now spattering on the wind-screen. I put on the lights, on dip, the sun having dug itself into that dirty black cloud, and got itself lost.

In my rear-vision mirror were two

headlights on main beam, when all that was needed was dipped heads. I slowed to allow him to pass, edging across until my nearside tyres were scrubbing in the grass verge. We were now out into the countryside of Shropshire.

Still he came on, and suddenly was alongside me, edging closer and now dropping his speed. There was a thump and a judder through the steering wheel—his front nearside wheel had nudged our front wing. And then he fell back again. The dogs were now wide awake and barking.

'Richard!' Amelia cried out. But I was too busy trying to attribute the incident to pure bad driving.

I'd been able to spare enough time to realise that this looked very like Harry Martin's Land Rover. I could see nothing of the person behind the steering wheel, as he—or she—was sitting higher than me, and was the other side of the Land Rover.

Now the black cloud had swallowed the sun completely, which didn't help at all.

But the headlights were still there, behind me. I tried one or two of the obvious manoeuvres, either to draw ahead, or to slow and allow the Land Rover to lead, but with no noticeable effect. We would do half a mile, with the headlights stubbornly in the rear-view mirror, then I would accelerate a little for a mile or so—but still the Land Rover hung on, waiting for the opportunity . . . to do what? What on earth was going on?

'Richard!' Amelia complained. 'Pull over and let him get ahead, if that's what he wants.' She had been staring back over her shoulder.

But *was* that what he wanted? There was something taunting about the Land Rover's manoeuvres, something threatening.

It appeared to be the time to employ my meagre knowledge of stunt-driving. At one time—years ago it seemed, thinking back to that time—I had taken an advanced driving course with police patrol cars, during which I had learned tricks with a car that I had never guessed were possible. The situation now arose in which this minor ability might at last be useful, as I seemed to have encountered one of those driving lunatics who caused nothing but trouble to other drivers, even if unintentionally.

But this performance—and I had to cope with another hectic manoeuvre—was clearly intentional. If it *was* Harry's Land Rover, who was driving it and what did they want? I fought with the steering wheel, which was trying to jerk out of my hands.

The obvious thing to do was to pull in and wait until he disappeared into the distance, but a reserve of pride was nudging me. Who the hell did he think he was?

'Hold on,' I said. In the rear, the dogs were now whining. I had to divide my attention between the road borders and the Land Rover, and try to ignore Amelia's protests.

Then he came at me again. He had seemed to fall back, but apparently only in order to build up speed for the next nudge. I could remember no more than one trick that might help—the braked spin. I eased off the throttle and touched the brake, and he slid ahead, poised for another nudge.

It was then that I tried the handbrake spin. You do it by locking the rear wheels with the handbrake, but leaving the front wheels free, for steering. I was not certain that it would work with Amelia's car. But the road surface was now wet, and the rain was abruptly lashing down. It worked fine. Too well. Theoretically, I should have been facing the way we had come, but I rather overdid it, doing a full 360 degree spin, and finding myself heading again for Bridgnorth. The Land Rover had tried to nudge against my front wing, which had been no longer there to be nudged.

'Richard!' Amelia clutched my arm. It had been close to a scream. The dogs protested with a few yelps, but the Land Rover driver, having been completely confused, now had it nose-down in the nearside ditch. I braked to a halt, thought about it, then I reversed past it slowly, with a probing glance sideways. Yet nobody had climbed out, and I could not decide who was sitting there, behind the steering wheel, head down, forehead on the steering wheel rim.

I slowed to a crawl. Whoever it was could be seriously injured—even with a fractured skull. If not too hurt, he was about to hear my guess as to his parentage.

Amelia realised my intention, and said quickly, 'No, Richard. Let's get away from here. Away!'

Yet my training asserted itself. I could not desert someone who might be seriously injured, whether or not my action with Amelia's car could be described as self-defence. I wanted to know what was going on, anyway.

'I can't, love,' I said. 'Can't leave it like this.'

She said nothing, simply stared straight ahead, withdrawing herself completely from the scenario, and oozing disapproval.

I reversed back and stopped, then got out of the car. The grass verge here was extensive and flat, a good ten yards wide, but the stricken Land Rover was nose-down, most deeply on its near side, into what turned out to be a very deep ditch, tucked tight beneath the hedgerow. Its headlights were still operating, and the light was reflected as an eerie green. The driver's head rested against the steering wheel, and a shock of hair was draped over it. A woman, then?

There was only a very little light from the headlights, which were dug into the grass bank, and I was hesitant about taking any action that might do more damage than good.

But there was one thing I could do. I reached inside, the driver's window being wound down, and released the door lock. As I swung open the door, having to lift its weight, Amelia appeared at my side, torch in hand. The sun was rapidly failing us.

'It's a woman,' I said to her. The driver's auburn hair hung forward, like a curtain, over the wheel. I put a hand beneath it and threw it back, as Amelia's torchlight fell directly on the driver's head.

'It's Penny,' I said. Amelia was silent. 'Penny Downes,' I put it more accurately, partly to myself because I was having difficulty in accepting it.

'Yes,' Amelia whispered. 'I see. There's blood, Richard.'

'I know.'

A single drop had just fallen from the rim of the wheel and on to the driver's knee. Another drip was forming on her chin, and the curtain of hair fell forward again. She mumbled something, but not in distinguishable words. Gently, carefully, I reached across and swept her hair back again, out of her face. Now, in the dimly reflected light, I could see that her forehead had struck the rim of the steering wheel. The wound was an inch above her right eyebrow, blood running down her cheek and into the corner of her stubbornly closed mouth, then out of it, and down her chin.

Behind me, traffic was whipping past, headlights briefly splashing over us. But nobody stopped in order to ask whether we needed help. An ambulance, for instance. I was glad of that. It would need a complex explanation in order to justify the situation—nothing, in any event, that I could invent with confidence.

She moaned, and mumbled something. I bent close to her. It was clearly necessary to discover the extent of the damage.

'There's a cut on your forehead,' I told her quietly. 'No damage to your face that I can see. We'll take you home.'

'No,' she whispered. 'Not there.'

'Our home, I meant. Do you think you can get out and walk a few yards?'

No seat-belt in the Land Rover, I realised. Otherwise, perhaps, there would not have been any damage to her forehead.

'I'll try,' she whispered.

So, with my arm around her, as far as I could reach, hand as comfortable as possible around her waist, I tried to lift her up the steeply sloped seat. She sighed a groan, but I could not see how I might be hurting her.

'My leg,' she mumbled.

'Try,' I instructed, and she nodded.

'All right, then. Oops-a-daisy.'

She couldn't have weighed above eight stone. With my thigh wedged against the door frame, I managed to lift her clear of the seat, but then I nearly lost my centre of effort, my foot beginning to slide forward into the ditch.

'Can you reach her legs out?' I asked Amelia. 'Reach past. Can you do it, d'you think?' She nodded.

I had no way of knowing whether Penny had any damage to her legs. She was wearing jeans. I had to pray that she had not. Already I had flouted the basic rules for this situation, which included flagging down a passing car, and asking them to phone the police and get an ambulance. And the police. It seemed to me that official intervention was not what we needed. In fact, it would seriously complicate the situation. I wanted to find out what she'd been playing at—what she was doing with Harry's Land Rover—without the interference of anyone else just yet.

By then, Amelia, kneeling in the wet grass, had managed to reach out a leg, manoeuvring it very carefully. I rotated Penny on the seat, so that the other leg could be freed. She moaned. I said, 'Hold on, nearly there, now.' Then, with both her feet on the ground, I was able to raise her to her full height. The rain was now lashing down.

'Can you walk?' I asked her.

She managed a stumble in the thick grass. With my arm round her waist, taking most of the weight from her legs, and her arm round my neck, she was able to move, whimpering, as Amelia went ahead to hold open the passenger's front door of her own car. The dogs, eager to discover what was happening, tried to climb over from the rear, but I gave them a couple of sharp commands, to which they were not accustomed, and they returned to their rear seat, sulking.

I slid Penny on to the front passenger's seat, and went round to the driver's door. From her direction, Amelia could now slide Penny's legs across as I reached for the seat-belt. She whimpered, and thrust my hand away. Behind me, Amelia was busy trying to calm the dogs, as she slid between them. They were not used to having Amelia with them on their rear seat, and were being over-affectionate with their welcome.

Then I went back to take the keys from the Land Rover, switch off its lights, and reach across for Penny's shoulder bag. It felt rather heavy. Back in the car, Amelia was now settled, with a dog each side of her, and trying very hard to restrain them. She didn't use much make-up, but whatever there was, they had it off in a few seconds. The tongues of two full-grown boxers could cover quite an area in no time at all.

Penny was leaning forward, her face in her hands, and moaning. Amelia said, 'There're tissues in the glove compartment,' and with a sob Penny fumbled for the box, but not touching it.

'I'm bleeding,' she complained, in a voice

not far from hysteria.

'Tissues,' said Amelia again, and with almost a burst of anger, as though it was all our fault, Penny snatched the box.

'Just above your right eyebrow,' Amelia told her.

Cautiously, Penny applied a pad of tissues to her brow, then stared at the result. It was too dark for her to see anything, so I put on the inside light.

'Let me see,' I offered.

She turned her head away. 'No.'

I shrugged, switched off the inside light, and started the engine, checked the road behind me, and cautiously backed on to the tarmac surface.

'What're you doing?' Penny asked anxiously, spitting out bits of tissue.

'Taking you home,' I told her. 'Our home. To attend to that properly.'

'I don't want—'

I cut her off sharply. You can take so much aggravation—no more. 'It's got nothing to do with what you want,' I told her. 'We can't leave you with the Land Rover.'

'I don't want—'

'Be quiet,' I said sharply. 'Fasten your seatbelt—we don't need to know what you do or don't want.' I had to say it twice before it penetrated.

She sat back, sniffling now into a handful of tissues.

We were only about four miles from Bridgnorth. There would, at that time, be a certain amount of congestion at the bridge, so I took the turn-off at the top of Hermitage Hill, picked up the road from Kidderminster, and turned right. We could now skirt the town, and very soon I was able to turn off into our own lane. I headed for our parking area.

'We're here,' I said. 'Can you get out without help?'

CHAPTER EIGHT

As I might have expected, Mary came hurrying out, in spite of the rain, and before I had time to snap open my seat-belt. She had flung a mac over her head.

'Richard! I've been so worried.'

I slid out, put an arm round her shoulders, and squeezed her comfortingly. 'Mary, you ought to know by now—I'm always getting mixed up with something or other. Now get back inside, before you catch a chill.'

She ignored that.

Amelia managed to reach across the dogs and open both rear doors. Otherwise, they would have trampled all over her, in order to tell Mary they were back. Then Amelia was able to get out herself.

'Oh, Mary! You'll never guess —'

'Amelia, my love,' said Mary, 'I don't have to guess. Go inside and get yourself dry. The fire's on in the sitting-room. And who's this you've brought to visit us?'

It was not the time for formal introductions. 'I'll tell you all about it later, Mary,' I promised. 'Come on, Penny. Out you get.'

Amelia hesitated, until she was certain that I could manage alone, then ran for the open door.

'It's my leg,' whispered Penny.

'What's the matter with your leg?' Mary asked.

'Twisted it. And I've hurt my forehead,' Penny said miserably, then she clapped her palms to her face, and her shoulders heaved with sobs.

For a minute or two it became chaotic, with Mary trying to help Penny out of her seat, the dogs pushing in to see what was happening, and Penny, her hands clamped to her face, shivering and weeping, and interspersing a few cries of pain, unable to orientate herself to the over-spill of attention, in which the dogs took a substantial part.

'A bit of an accident,' I said quietly to Mary. 'She's got a wound on her forehead. Banged it on a steering wheel, and maybe she's twisted a leg. But the thing is to get her inside, and some dry clothes on her . . . and then we'll see . . . sort out a few matters.'

'An accident, Richard?' Mary asked. 'You don't have accidents.'

I put an arm round her shoulders. 'This time, I've really got an excuse, Mary. The young lady tried to force us off the road—'

'What! The wicked thing!'

'But she came off worse,' I told her. 'Now . . . she's soaked through and shivering. It's probably partly shock. Will you and Amelia introduce her to a nice hot bath, and try to find something dry to put on her? I've got to make a phone call.'

'You're all wet, Richard,' Mary told me severely. 'You're not to stand about in those clothes.'

I grunted agreement, then walked into the hall, where Amelia and Penny had paused at the foot of the stairs. Penny turned her head, and flung her hair from her face with the back of a hand. 'What phone call?' she demanded.

So she had heard. Her voice was now more firm. She was recovering her self-control.

'Well . . .' I said. 'To the police, of course.'

'The police . . .' Her hand flew to her mouth. 'Why? What . . .'

'The police,' I insisted. 'And you know damned well why. I'll be down here, love,' I explained to Amelia. 'Making a phone call.'

'I heard you,' said Amelia. 'Now come along, Penny. A really hot bath will make you feel much better, and we'll look at that leg, shall we?' She put a hand on Penny's arm, but she shook it off. 'And you too, Richard. Get out of those clothes. You'll catch a chill.'

'In a minute, love. The phone . . .'

Then Amelia urged our guest up the staircase, although Penny kept appealing for more information about my threatened phone call, and hanging back. To help things along, I said, 'I've got to report a motoring incident.'

Which produced a choked protest from Penny. And Mary added a final, bitter comment.

'Sheba's limping. Right foreleg.'

142

'Oh hell!' I said, but to myself. Gradually, any remaining sympathy for Penny, in her tricky situation, was fluttering away. I could, now, with the slightest possible provocation, have happily put Penny over my knees, and tanned the spirit right out of her.

Angrily, and before Penny could disappear beyond hearing distance, I walked over to our hall phone, on its little table by the front door, grabbed it up, and dialled 999. 'Police, please,' I requested, when I got a response, and behind me, from our small landing at the head of the stairs, there was a choked plea, 'Oh no . . .'

'Now come along,' said Amelia, taking her arm. But Penny hung back, clinging to the banister.

'Oh no,' she whispered again. I could just hear it.

'Oh yes,' I said, over my shoulder. Then the line connected. 'Is that the police?'

'Yes, sir. Can we help you? Trouble, is it? If it's urgent—'

But I cut him off short, a glance up the stairs confirming that Amelia had now introduced Penny to our bathroom, but had not yet closed the door.

'Not urgent.' I raised my voice a little. 'Just a bit of information.'

'Very well, sir. If you'll give me a moment . . .'

'Certainly.'

I was still trying to adapt to the advances in technology that the police seemed to have acquired since my time with them.

'Now, sir . . .'

He was going to record it on tape—so much easier and more reliable than trying to get it down in shorthand, as in my days.

'I've just driven in from Wolverhampton,' I said. 'There's a deserted Land Rover, nose-in to a ditch. I took the keys out of the ignition lock, to stop it getting stolen, so if you'd send somebody along, I'll hand them over.' Not a single lie in it, I thought.

'Yes, sir. And your address please.'

I told him. 'Beeches Lane—you'll know it.' Without having to look round, I was aware that Amelia and Penny were listening to what I was saying, with every nerve strained.

'We'll send someone along,' said the desk officer. 'Thank you.'

I hung up, and turned. There was now no sign of either Amelia or Penny. I heard the bathroom door close. It makes a bit of a squeak against a raised edge of lino. So I wandered into the kitchen, hoping that Mary was considering brewing a pot of tea. As, of course, she was, because she already had a kettle singing, and was laying out cups and saucers.

'Make mine a mug,' I told her. 'Hot and sweet.'

She gave me a small grimace, which might have been intended as a smile. 'As though I don't know.' Then, her back to me, she said,

'Tell me, Richard. Before they come down. What's happened?'

I called Sheba to me, recalling her minor limp. She obediently, and without prompting, put her paw in my hand, and I gently massaged it. There was very little wrong, as she made no sound and no attempt to snatch it free. As she always over-reacted to any hurt or clumsy treatment, I knew that her difficulty was minor. So I gave her back her paw, and she limped away, making a show of it, seeking sympathy. Dogs are like children. Jake sat and watched, with his head cocked. There had been no damage to him, but he envied Sheba the attention.

There seemed to be insufficient time in which to tell Mary the full story, so I gave her a quick outline of it, as we waited for the other two to join us.

'But *why*, Richard?' she asked. 'Why would she do such a wicked thing?'

'Now that,' I told her, 'is what I'm going to try to find out. I can guess, but guesses are never any use.'

'I can't believe a girl would do a thing like that on purpose ...'

I took off my jacket and Mary hung it over the back of a chair. My trousers seemed to be wet only around my ankles, where the cuffs had dragged in the wet grass. I turned up the bottom six inches, which seemed to help, but still there were the wet stockings.

'You'll have to change your socks,' Mary told me. 'Your house slippers are over there, by the fridge.'

There were no dry socks within reach, and I couldn't go upstairs and break in on Amelia and Penny. But bare feet, when towelled, and in dry slippers, felt much more comfortable. I was beginning to feel almost human again. In fact, if the degree of comfort raised itself by only a few notches, I knew that my anger at Penny's extraordinary—even callous—actions would rapidly cool.

I lit my pipe. A mug of tea, hot and strong and sweet, appeared at my elbow on the kitchen table, as Amelia walked in, ushering Penny ahead of her.

There was no doubt that the girl was much chastened. Although she was about twenty-six years old, her obvious mental immaturity demanded that she should be called a girl, and this girl was very frightened. I knew, then, that Amelia hadn't wasted her time in the bathroom with Penny, and had no doubt stressed the matter of my being an ex-inspector of police, and exaggerated my standing with the local force. Probably, she would also have warned her about my violent reactions to the kind of behaviour that Penny had been presenting. In other words, Penny would be terrified, even before I could tell her what I thought about her.

As it happened, I was at the open front

146

door, having answered the door bell, when they came down, looking remarkably like sisters, with Penny wearing a selection from Amelia's wardrobe. They were very like each other in height and build. The police had wasted no time. A uniformed constable was standing in the porch.

'Are you Mr Patton . . . oh, sorry, sir. Of course you are. You won't remember me. I was a rookie when you left us. Tomlinson, sir.'

'I remember you,' I told him. 'You've come for the keys, I suppose.' I handed them over. 'It's the Land Rover, about four miles—'

'Yes, sir,' he interrupted. 'There's a team there, right now.'

'Then there's some information I can give you. But come inside. There was mention of a cup of tea . . .'

He followed me into the kitchen. There seemed to be no harm in giving Penny a worry or two. She needed the lesson. I therefore kept my eyes on her as the constable entered. She turned away abruptly, at the sight of the uniform. Mary was reaching out another cup and saucer.

Tomlinson stood there politely, one hand on the table, the other loosely at his side, where Sheba could reach his fingers and lick them. Tomlinson looked down, and fondled an ear. Jake uncurled himself from his warm corner, and went to smell the mood—friendly or not—of this visitor.

'When you get back to your inspector,' I told Tomlinson, 'you can give him the information that the Land Rover belonged to a man named Harry Martin. A phone call to the Wolverhampton police will get you all the facts. Harry Martin was killed last night.'

Tomlinson flicked his eyes around, perhaps searching for information in our expressions. Penny moved across to where Sheba was now lying down, and gently fondled her left front paw. No reaction. I thought I heard Penny sigh. Tomlinson said, 'You mean . . . no, it can't fit. I thought for a second that you meant he was killed in that Land Rover.'

'No. Indeed not. The Land Rover must have been stolen from where he'd parked it. That was in the small car-park at Tettenhall. Martin was killed with something hard and heavy. A blow to the head. No connection, I'd say, to the theft of the Land Rover and its crash into the ditch. I remember noting that he'd left his keys in the ignition lock.'

'Yes, sir,' said the constable. 'I'll pass it on. Well, I'd better be off.' He nodded around, spared a special smile for Penny, and left us. Amelia went with him to see him out.

For a couple or so minutes there was silence in the kitchen. Mary, seeing that we were all supplied with tea, reached up into her special cupboard, fastened to the wall, and produced her first-aid kit.

'Come and sit under the light,' she told

Penny. 'So that we can see what we're doing.'

Uneasily, Penny complied.

'Lift your head,' said Mary. 'Let's get a good look at your forehead first. Your legs seem all right.'

By this time, the wound above Penny's right eye had nearly ceased to bleed, but her own efforts with tissues had not enhanced her appearance. Although she had washed off the blood that had smeared her cheek and her chin, she had clearly left her forehead well alone—perhaps it was too painful, or perhaps she had been afraid of starting the bleeding again. It was not a pretty sight.

'Clean you up first,' said Mary, reaching for cotton wool and one of her magic bottles. Surgical spirit, the label on the bottle informed me. 'There,' she said after a while, 'that's looking better. It's just the cut over your right eye that's tricky.'

An antiseptic smell now filled the kitchen. To me, when I moved closer, it seemed to be more than a mere cut. It wasn't far from requiring stitches. But I didn't say anything. Stitches would mean a doctor or a hospital, as Mary was equipped with neither the necessary equipment, nor the training. But she had her own techniques, involving two strips of sticking plaster, one above the wound, one below, and crossing strips to draw the edges together.

'There,' she said. 'See your own doctor as soon as you can.'

But Penny's expression remained blank. She was no doubt considering that she had to see her parents, sometime or other, and possibly that evening. Perhaps she would be able to explain her injury as a motor-cycle accident, but in that event there would be an outcry against her riding, in future, behind Philip on his bike. If so, Philip would not be pleased with her. Her activities, in fact, if she chose to tell him the truth, would certainly be greeted with a degree of outrage.

Penny could see trouble ahead. I was intending to start things off, in that sphere, and very shortly.

Normally we would, at this time, be preparing for our main meal of the day—dinner. This, Mary would already be close to serving, and though we did not specifically dress for dinner, certainly I would need a change, if only because I wanted to get out of my damp suit.

'Then don't be long, Richard,' Amelia said.

'Time for a bath, is there?' I asked.

Mary looked to Amelia for that answer. Amelia said, 'Time for it, though I reckon the water will only be warm.'

'Hmph!' I said, and I headed for the stairs, wondering why women seemed to need more water to wallow in than men.

She was quite correct about the shortage of hot water. I was in and out as fast as I could manage, and, far from dressing for dinner, I undressed, as one might put it. A clean shirt, my old and comfortable slacks, clean socks, and my suede shoes. I was feeling much better.

As I walked down the stairs, I saw that Penny was using our phone. She failed to hear me coming, and her voice was raised in what seemed to be a spurt of anger.

'Then ask! It's called The Beeches, and I reckon everybody around here knows the name. Patton. Yes.' A pause. 'I'll tell you, Philip. But not over the phone. And bring my riding kit. I can't *wait* to get away from here.' A pause again. 'And the same to you.' She slammed down the phone.

Coming down the stairs, from behind her, I said, 'You don't seem satisfied with our hospitality.'

She turned. 'Oh hell! Sorry.'

'You're having a full day of it, aren't you! Apologies scattered all over the place. And now you want to rush away. Frightened that I want to find out just what you think you were up to, I suppose.'

Her eyes were hunting, right and left, searching for a way out. She stood there, feet apart to give her the best balance, her fists clenched, and if the jut of her jaw meant anything, I realised that it would be difficult to get an explanation out of her against her will.

She decided to have done with that subject. 'We're eating in the kitchen, I'm told.'

'Yes.'

'Do you always do that?' It was no more than a quest for knowledge.

'Yes,' I told her. 'Unless somebody important visits us. And as there's nobody important—'

'All right,' she cut in. 'I get your point. Mary . . . it's Mary, isn't it?' She waited for my nod. 'Mary told me to fetch you. A good job you're not still in the bath.'

Now she was going all coy on me. It didn't suit her. She saw me, of course, as the person who might drop her right into trouble, if I told the full story of the Land Rover to my friends in the police force. She had to work hard, in order to get me on her side. She had realised that, but she couldn't guess that the more effort she put into it, the more I distrusted the sincerity she was trying to project.

'I think,' I said, 'that there's a lot of explaining to do. But not now. Amelia will be calling for us any minute, and what I have to say will be better said without interruption, and on a full stomach.'

She did a little wander around the hall, glancing out of the window, which overlooked our parking patch, and shrugged. I could make a fair guess that she was hoping for Philip's appearance, on his Suzuki, at any minute now. She was quite prepared to forgo a dinner, if she could get away from The Beeches. Away from me. It was with more than a hint of enjoyment that I watched her. If she was so

152

anxious to get away, then she was quite aware that I had a few simple questions to ask her, and that they would be difficult to answer. Well . . . more than simple questions, I realised, as I weighed up my plans. Interrogation, that was what I intended, something much more than a basic quest for information . . . a demand, rather.

The dinner was of course, as usual, splendid. Amelia decided that we ought to have wine with it, something we usually did only for special occasions. All right, so this was a special occasion. Didn't we have with us the district's expert at ditching Land Rovers? But Penny rejected the wine. She was very depressed, and kept glancing out of the window. It would do her no good, as that window did not offer a view of our parking patch. She kept her head cocked, but Mary and Amelia were chattering away, completely ignoring her, and overwhelming any sound of a Suzuki arriving.

At last, the meal finished, Penny came to her feet, as the rest of us did, then she looked somewhat lost, wondering whether she ought to help with the washing-up, in which event she might miss not only the sound of Philip's arrival, but also the sight. I put a hand to her arm, quite lightly, and led her out into the hall.

'The sitting-room,' I said. 'We're going to do some sitting, and some talking, you and I.'

'I don't feel like—'

I cut her off. 'Nevertheless, you're going to do some talking, young lady. Yes, that's right. Follow my wife. That's fine. Now, just stand there . . . Amelia, will you come and stand with Penny? I think she's feeling a bit shy. Isn't that so, Penny? Although, come to think about it, she's got every reason to be.'

'To be what?' Amelia asked, frowning.

'Shy, my love. Frankly, if I was in her situation, I'd feel really worried.'

'Now . . . Richard—'

I winked at her, and she looked away. I was moving one of the winged easy chairs to a position facing the window. It seemed necessary to be able to interpret any variation in Penny's expression.

'What's going on?' she asked.

'You sit there,' I told her. 'I'm going to sit facing you. And my wife and Mary can sit anywhere behind you.'

'What're you going to do?' Penny looked round at Mary and Amelia, getting no more than a shrug from Mary and a shake of the head from Amelia. They didn't understand what I intended, and Mary merely fluffed up the cushions, to make a comfortable nest of it.

'Fine,' I said. 'Now . . . sit,' I instructed Penny, pointing to the prepared chair.

She sat, as upright as she could manage, lifted her chin, and stared at me with defiance. I moved an ordinary dining-chair from a corner, turned it backwards, and sat astride it.

154

In this way, I could hook my fingers on the back of it, and rest my chin on the knuckles, when necessary. We stared eye-to-eye, six feet between us, and, as far as Penny was concerned, a considerable dark cloud of animosity.

'Well, get on with it,' she said. 'Whatever it is.'

'Now that we've all eaten and have calmed down a bit, I'm going to ask you some questions, and I expect straight answers,' I told her, nodding seriously.

For several moments she stared unblinkingly at me. Then she said, 'Expect what you like. I'm not going to say anything.'

CHAPTER NINE

For a whole minute, as far as I could mentally calculate, I allowed the silence to build up. Then I said, 'Yes?'

'Yes what?' she demanded.

'I'm sorry. I thought you said something.'

'No.' She shook her head, her hair flying. 'No, No!'

'Then don't you think,' I asked her, in a tone I considered to be quite reasonable, 'that it's about time you did?'

'About what?'

I could tell that even this small interchange of words was proving to be a strain on her. Her attempt at baffled innocence was pitifully poor. She was wriggling herself into the cushions behind her, trying to convey a casual lack of anything resembling involvement.

'Very well,' I said. 'It seems that I'll have to do a little prompting. Not acceptable in a court of law, of course. But here . . . well, I can ask what I like. Such as leading questions.'

She shrugged, pouted, and said, 'All right. Ask away.' Then she turned and looked at Amelia for encouragement. But Amelia had been in the car; she was not someone to whom Penny might appeal, and expect support. So she switched her concentration, now, to Mary, who nodded to her and said, 'And make sure

156

you answer them, or you'll have to answer to me.'

I could not understand, myself, what Mary meant by that, but she managed to convey the impression that interrogation by me would be a meek and paltry experience, compared with having to submit to Mary's technique.

I made an attempt at a smile, but it failed, and there was a snap in my voice when I'd organised the words in my mind. But Penny had said, Ask away. So this I proceeded to do.

'Why did you try to force us off the road?' I asked, quite crisply I thought.

Penny shrugged. 'It was only a hint.' She was almost whispering, her voice was so strictly controlled.

'I can take hints,' I assured her. 'You could have come to me and said, "Can I give you a hint?" And I'd have said, "Yes, of course you can. Go ahead." And you could have given me the hint, there and then, and saved yourself the trouble of having to steal the Land Rover.'

'Oh yes!' Penny managed a tone of disgusted lack of belief. 'I'd have gone to you—six feet of muscle, and not much good at understanding—walked up to you and told you to clear off, I suppose! Don't tell me you'd have listened. Yah! I don't believe a word of it.'

I flicked a glance at Amelia, who was trying not to smile, her face stiff with the effort.

'Oh,' I assured Penny, 'I'd have listened.

Not necessarily gone along with what you had to say, which, I gather, would have been a straightforward demand for me to clear off and leave it all to you. But I'd have listened.'

Penny frowned. She was seriously and sincerely considering it. Then she said, 'Something like that. I did catch a word or two. What you were saying—to your wife.' She turned, and smiled at Amelia, perhaps apologising for eavesdropping.

'What I was saying?' I asked. 'I don't remember saying anything that could have angered you. Or even upset you.'

She shook her head. Experience had taught her how effective that swirl of auburn hair could be. Then she looked down at her hands, clasped in her lap, and up again. 'You were being a nuisance, that's what.'

'Ah . . .' I said, and I glanced at Amelia, raising my eyebrows. She shrugged. Nothing was becoming clear and logical, so I tried another aspect to present to Penny.

'In what way was I being a nuisance?' I asked. 'Go on. Tell me. I've got quite a thick skin.'

'Putting your nose in, when it was none of your business.'

There was then a pause. I had to marshal my thoughts. 'What was none of my business?' I asked at last, carefully, not really expecting a solid and reasonable response.

Penny shrugged, stared at her fingernails,

and confided to her lap. 'You're digging it all up again, aren't you? Go on—deny it. If you dare.' Then she lifted her head in defiance.

I could see that Amelia had her hand to her lips. Did she find this amusing? I wondered.

'Yes,' I said, nodding. 'I'm digging it all up again . . .'

'There! You see. You're admitting it.'

'Admitting?' I asked, wondering now who was questioning whom. 'Well . . . of course. As I've already told you, Connie's asked me to try to prove that it wasn't she who killed Sylvia Thomas, on that terrible night of the storm, ten years ago. Now . . . that isn't something that you've got to put a stop to, before I find out the truth . . .' I paused. 'Is it?'

Her hands had been clasped around her chin and her cheeks. Now she drew them apart. 'How do I know?' she demanded. 'How *could* I know?'

'I can't think of an answer to that,' I admitted. 'But now, of course, we've got another death—Harry's. Philip's father. He's dead.'

Then suddenly she flung her arms around wildly. 'I didn't want you messing around and making a botch of everything—like you did before. You and your detecting!' She tailed off with a snort of disgust.

'To what are you—'

She cut in smartly. 'Oh don't put it on. All correct grammar and a nice, lofty voice.

Hiding away . . .' She paused, staring at me with contempt. 'Go on, deny it. Try and persuade me you *really* believed that Connie had killed that bitch, Sylvia Thomas. I just don't believe any of it. Of *course* she didn't. And now, what're you doing? You've got another one to play around with . . .' She held up a hand, realising I was about to burst in. 'Another murder. Harry's. And if you get anywhere near that, I bet you'll make just as big a botch of it as you did last time. With Connie. And you're wondering why I tried to shove you off the road! *Now* do you see? I didn't want you making a balls-up of this one, too.' She paused, looking around at Amelia and Mary. 'If you two can't keep him under control, and tell him to drop it and stay at home, because he'll only make a mess of Harry's death, too . . . then *I've* got to do something.'

'Now wait . . .' Amelia tried to put in. But I lifted two fingers from the chair back. She understood, and was at once silent.

'Are you telling me,' I asked Penny, 'that you tried to run us off the road, just to stop me from investigating Harry's death?'

'Yes. It's what I said.' And again there was that toss of the head, that swirl of the hair.

'You tried to kill us,' I challenged her, presenting a worst-case scenario.

'You were getting to be a nuisance.' She was persisting with it, but she had not denied my charge.

'Hmm!' I said. 'Then am I to believe that you try to kill anyone who's a nuisance—anyone who gets in your way?'

'No! No, that's stupid.'

'Or just me.'

'Not kill. No. You're not to say that.' She was now becoming agitated, losing control of her equanimity. 'Only frighten a bit.'

'Frighten *me* then,' I persisted. She was becoming so incensed that I felt she might make a slip in her declarations. 'I don't frighten easily.'

She shrugged. 'It wasn't so important, anyway.'

'So . . .' I said, 'if it *had* been important, you'd have tried harder?'

'It wasn't all *that* important.' She grimaced. There was impatience in her expression—she was repeating herself, now.

'What wasn't?' I asked, interested.

'Important to you,' she said heavily, annoyed with me. 'Important enough for you to stick your vardy in.'

'My what?'

'Your nose, then. Sniffing around for clues.'

I stole a quick glance at Amelia and Mary. There was no evidence in their expressions that they knew, any better than I did, what Penny was talking about.

'Clues?' I asked. 'Are you talking about Harry's death?'

'Who else is there?' Penny demanded. 'What other death do you know about, when I've heard nothing?'

I sighed. Penny was presenting herself as a member of that unique group of people who can never follow a straight line of logic. I could easily imagine her, in a witness box, reducing a barrister almost to tears of sheer frustration.

'I don't know of any other death,' I told her. 'And frankly, I don't know much about Harry's death. Only that he is dead, and that the blow to his head was very like the blow that killed Sylvia Thomas.'

'How do you know that?' she demanded.

'Oh dear . . .' I sighed. 'It was my case: the death of Sylvia Thomas. I can recall that contusion on the crown of her head. All weapons leave their own specific signs,' I told her, as though I might be lecturing a group of trainee coppers. 'And—as I said—the contusion . . . you *do* know what a contusion is?' I asked her.

She nodded. 'I know.'

'Well . . . that's something.'

She shrugged. 'I was training to be a nurse. We had lectures.'

'Hmm!' I considered her expression, the defiant light in her eyes and her jutting lower lip, and wondered why she was not, therefore, a nurse. But I could now hazard a guess that she would not be sufficiently patient; would fail her examinations because she found herself with reservations as to the expert contents of her textbooks. Her clumsy and ineffectual attempt to treat her own wound indicated an impatience that would not be welcome on the wards.

'Well,' I said, 'at least you know what a contusion is. So you'll be interested in the fact that the contusion on Sylvia Thomas's head, in so far as I can remember it, was very like the contusion on Harry's head. Exactly the same spot on the crown of his head.'

She stared at me with her head cocked, then burst out, as though the image had leapt out before her! 'Sort of—they were hit with the same chunk of wood . . . or whatever? Here . . . have you thought of this? There were lots of chunks of wood broken off and tossed around by that flood, and there was quite a wind last night—so there'd have been broken branches lying around . . .' She allowed this to tail off, in the face of my obvious scepticism.

'Oh,' I said, 'I expect there were, lots of branches. But you couldn't have been listening. Or you completely missed the point I wished to make.'

'Oh yes? And what was that?'

'The interesting fact that two random chunks of wood, or branches, one possibly thrown up by the flood waters of the River Severn, and one broken from the trees a matter of fifteen miles away—at Tettenhall— could match up so accurately that the contusions were alike.'

Again the swirl of her hair, again the defiant grimace. 'You're just *saying* that, as though that makes it a fact.'

I was toying, here, with improbabilities, hoping she would not realise it. We had known that Sylvia Thomas had been killed with the rolling-pin, which just happened to be convenient. The contusion had been round, and its diameter lined up with the diameter of the rolling-pin, and there had been blood on it, which the technicians identified as belonging to Sylvia Thomas. But now, we were dealing with an entirely different proposition. Again, the contusion to Harry's head was to the crown, and it had been viciously murderous. But there could be no suggestion that a smooth and round weapon had killed Harry. Certainly, it was clear that nothing remotely resembling the smooth roundness and diameter of a rolling-pin was responsible in this case. So . . . for me to connect Harry's death to Sylvia Thomas's by way of the weapon would be fallacious, and I could tell from Penny's expression that she knew it.

There was now just a tiny smile on her lips. She had realised that I'd talked myself into a non-valid position.

'I don't know why you're telling me this,' she said placidly. 'I don't know much about the death of that other person—and that's only from what Philip's told me—so why we're talking about it, I can't imagine.'

'Then you have a very poor imagination, Penny,' I told her. 'Or a very vivid one that's leading you astray. Is *that* why you tried to frighten us—both my wife and myself—by shunting us off the road? Something as simple as your own hectic imagination?'

'Not frighten. Just discourage.'

'All right,' I accepted, as blandly as I could make it. 'Discourage. But why? Why, Penny, should it matter to you what I might be thinking?'

She was silent for a full minute. At last she managed to make a dismissive gesture.

'From what Philip's told me, it's obvious you made a right mess of that prostitute's death. I don't want you making another.'

I smiled at her. 'Then we ought to get together, you and me, because we're of a like mind on this. Neither of us wants any mistakes. Me because I believe I made mistakes last time—with Sylvia Thomas's death. And *you* don't want any mistakes about Harry's death?'

She bit her lip, and nodded.

'Because you think I've got my eye on your Philip?' I asked.

She nodded again, reluctant to resort to words. 'And if I tell you I haven't . . .'

'Then you'd be lying.' And she nodded emphatically, hair flying again.

'In that case I won't even suggest the possibility.'

She frowned. 'I don't know what you mean,' she admitted reluctantly.

'I'm saying—to please you—that I haven't got my eye on Philip, as being the murderer of Harry, his father.'

It seemed that nothing would satisfy her. 'Why not?' she demanded.

'I will, if you like,' I offered.

'Now you're being funny.'

'No, I'm not,' I assured her. 'Think about it. Put it like this. Philip is more than likely the main beneficiary of his father's will. I don't know how much Harry is worth—I don't know whether Philip knows either—but it's a motive, isn't it? In any event, Connie wouldn't be entitled to the lion's share . . .'

But she was ahead of me. 'He couldn't completely disinherit his wife. I do know that much.'

'Connie was not his wife,' I told her. 'They were divorced. I'm surprised you don't know that. No doubt—though you'll have to allow for the fact that I don't know much civil law— but no doubt she *could* be disinherited. Will have been, she'll probably discover, when she's seen a solicitor. So . . . it will more than likely turn out that Philip is his father's only beneficiary. And wouldn't that be exciting? For both Philip and yourself. Had you realised that?'

She was not going to concede it. 'No. What do I know about the law . . . or about what

166

Harry had done about his will?'

'I don't know much civil law, Penny,' I admitted. 'I'd imagine that you know even less. But Connie's told me that she and Harry were divorced. So that means that he *could* have disinherited her completely, which would mean . . .' I shrugged. 'I'm not at all sure what the situation would be.'

She threw her hair back with a hand, and pouted. 'So why don't we wait and see?'

'Good idea.'

'But I'm quite sure . . .' She leaned forward in order to add emphasis to her remark. '. . . quite sure that Philip's not going to be running around, trying to discover what he's going to get out of his father's death.' She grimaced, expressing disgust. 'He's not like that.'

'One would hope not,' I offered. 'There's nothing so distasteful as a family scrambling around over a legacy.'

'I quite agree.' And Penny sat upright and tried to look dignified.

All of which did nothing to explain why she had driven us off the road. What—in other words—was it that she thought I might unearth, and would prove to be an embarrassment to her?

'That's him now,' she said suddenly, jerking upright and cocking her head.

'It's . . . oh, you mean Philip?' I thought I had detected a thrum of sound, abruptly silenced. Now there was a double pip from a motor-cycle horn.

Penny was on her feet. She ran to the window. 'It's Philip!'

'I did guess that,' I assured her. 'Shall we go and see whether he wants to take you away, or whether he's going to tell us we can keep you, as far as he's concerned?'

She was staring at me blankly. 'What the hell does that mean?' She had no sense of humour at all.

'He'll have driven past the abandoned Land Rover, if the police haven't winched it out and taken it away,' I explained. 'And he'll have guessed it was you who's left it in the ditch, if only because you've had to phone him from here. So he's likely to be very annoyed with you. I know I would be, if I was in his shoes. But why don't you go out to him? We don't want him marching in here with his riding boots on. Go on now, Penny. Do as you're told. It'll be a pleasant change for you. You'll enjoy it.'

She stared at me. 'You *do* know how to be unpleasant, don't you! An ex-copper! I suppose it's all I could expect. Is that part of your training?'

Once more there was the double pip of the horn. In a sudden panic, Penny said, 'I'll have to go and change. My stuff's upstairs.'

'Then do that,' I said. And Amelia added, 'Come along. Your own clothes should be dry now.'

'They are,' said Mary. 'I've ironed them and taken them upstairs. Come along. We mustn't keep him waiting.'

'No. I suppose not.' Penny was all in a flutter. Amelia said, 'We won't be long, Richard,' and they both got to their feet.

I nodded. Outside, the horn pipped again, so I obeyed its call and went out to speak to Philip Martin.

He had the bike leaning on its prop-stand and was waiting beside it, ferreting inside his anorak for his cigarettes, I saw, as he produced a pack.

'She won't be long,' I assured him.

He stood there, shrugged, and stared down at our steep garden, and over the river. 'Nice place you've got here.'

'It is, isn't it!' I agreed.

He was silent for a minute or two. Then he said, 'First the police ring me to tell me my dad's been found dead, and then she's on the phone, shouting a load of nonsense. What's the stupid creature been up to now?'

'Do you mean Penny?'

'You know I do, if you've been in her company for a couple of hours.' He managed to say this with a hint of pride.

I was filling my pipe. 'I wouldn't have said stupid. Impetuous, yes. Single-minded . . .'

'Stupid,' he insisted. 'What I've been hearing! Pinched my dad's Land Rover, of all things. And . . . doing what else? That's what I

169

want to know. Couldn't make sense out of it, over the phone.'

Probably not, I thought. He would have been shocked about his father, even though they were not close. Puzzled over why she had the Land Rover.

'Stupid creature,' he repeated. 'What did she expect me to do? Scare you off? If I've got the story right.'

'You have,' I told him. 'But it didn't work. She could have done some damage to your father's Land Rover, though.'

If there was anything on which I had failed to waste concern, it was the Land Rover. Let Penny sort it out with Philip.

'*My* Land Rover,' he corrected. 'Mine now.'

'Well, of course,' I agreed. 'I suppose it is. If you're Harry's only beneficiary, that is.'

He drew deeply on his cigarette. I watched him over the bowl of my pipe as I lit up. 'Are you?' I asked.

'Am I what?'

'Your father's only beneficiary.'

'Beneficiary. That's the word I don't understand,' he admitted. 'Those lawyers—I reckon they invent the words, just so you can't do without them . . . Beneficiary, for instance.'

'Oh . . . that,' I said. 'It's a person who inherits. Benefits, you see. Beneficiary. Get it? *Are* you the only one?' I asked him, cocking my head.

'Hah!' It was supposed to be a cynical laugh.

170

'You can't imagine him leaving anything to my mother, now can you! And if he did, I bet she'd throw it back in the solicitor's face. And there's nobody else but me.'

'Hmm!' I said. It didn't sound as if Philip had ever had a cosy family life, with his father more interested in womanising. And the past nine years, with Connie in prison, must have made him grow up very fast. But he had had the bungalow, as his own, for all those years, and he'd had Penny with him. He seemed to be the only one who benefited in this legal tangle.

'She's taking her time, isn't she!' He glanced at his watch.

'Women do,' I assured him. 'You ought to be used to that by now.'

'Haven't got all day.'

'You've got the rest of it.'

'You don't know anything about the things I've got to sort out,' he complained. 'I daren't go near a phone but what my mother rings me. It's as though she's got a private eye on the job, watching me, and reporting back to her. Wherever I happen to be, you can bet she reaches me, with her complaints, about how we've left the place. I'm getting right fed up with it, I can tell you that. How much crockery we've broken, how much nap we've worn off the carpets. Whatever nap is.'

And he slapped his driving gloves into his left hand. Slap-slap. I wondered whether he might be practising, in case he needed to put Penny over his knee. For a moment or two I was uncertain whether to advise him not to try it. But . . . to hell with it. Let him find out for himself what a spitfire she was . . . though he ought to know by now.

But perhaps he likes females with a bit of a spark in them. Not for him the compliant girls. Yes, Philip—no, Philip. That wasn't what he wanted in a woman. I hadn't asked him what he thought about Penny's theft and improper use of his Land Rover, and there was no point in asking him now. He would express himself differently to Penny than he would to me.

'Damn it,' he said, glancing at his watch. 'I thought you said she wouldn't be long.'

I shrugged. 'I got the impression that she couldn't wait to see you again.'

'She wouldn't trouble if I fell over this edge, here, and drowned myself.'

'But I would have something to say,' I assured him. 'You would ruin my garden.'

He peered over the edge. 'Is that a garden?'

'My hanging garden.'

'One of these days it's going to slide into the river.' He nodded sagely, as though he'd spent a lifetime studying steep gardens.

'It hasn't so far. Not a sign of it sliding,' I assured him.

And with similar useless dialogue, we filled in the time until Penny appeared. Then we had to wait while she climbed into her riding kit,

172

which Philip had brought for her. Leggings, I noticed, not over-trousers. With her crash-hat in place, she ceased to be Penny Downes, and became just his pillion rider.

She flung her shoulder bag over her head, so that it rested with a thud on her hip, then lifted herself on to the pillion seat.

Amelia was suddenly at my shoulder, slipping her hand round my arm. The engine fired. Penny raised a hand, signalling her goodbye.

We did not wave farewell to them. I think I sighed. It seemed that a great load had been lifted from my conscience. Let Philip take over, and try to cope with Penny, I thought. I did not envy him.

'A nice girl, really,' said Amelia.

'Umm!' I answered, glancing at her, wondering whether she really meant it.

CHAPTER TEN

There is something special about a house when the visitors have left. Even the closest of friends seem to intrude into the warm intimacy of a married couple—and of course, in our case, the additional presence of Mary.

'What a strange young lady,' Mary said, as I strolled into the kitchen, where Amelia and Mary had obviously been discussing Penny.

'It depends on what you mean by strange,' I said to Mary. 'There's certainly something about her that I can't understand. In that respect, she's strange. It's as though she's hiding part of her personality away, and offering the outside world only an edited version of herself.'

'Too subtle for me,' said Amelia. 'You imagine too much, Richard. It's not good for you.' She patted my cheek.

I shrugged. 'She steered all round it. Did you notice that?'

'All round what?'

'All round Harry's death,' I told her. 'And all round the details of Harry's will.'

'She'd be interested in that.' Amelia nodded firmly. 'After all, she's very close to Philip, and they've lived together for nearly ten years. Now . . . if Harry happens to have left a large sum of money, or negotiable assets—is that

174

what I mean?'

'It's what you mean,' I assured her. 'And it sounds feasible.'

'Yes,' she said. 'Well, if that's the case, then I'd guess that Penny will soon be urging Philip into thoughts of marriage.'

I grinned at her. 'Women always seem to be thinking about marriage.'

She did not take me up on that, concentration throwing a blanket over it. 'I wonder whether Connie will still offer them a roof over their heads,' she said, 'if they're married, and if Penny's eager for a family?'

'Quite frankly, love,' I said, 'Connie would feel she was in prison again, her freedom of movement threatened. She'd resent that.'

'Let's talk about something else, Richard,' she suggested. 'This is becoming depressing.'

'Yes. Let's do that. About what, though?'

'I'm surprised you haven't mentioned this yourself.' She pouted at me. 'I'd have thought you'd be eager to get to that Tettenhall place, and start asking questions about Harry's death. Have you lost interest in that?'

'Well . . . no. But who would there be to ask? And what questions?'

'It's not like you, Richard. Hesitating!'

I shrugged. 'The police . . . you'll remember what a sullen devil that Superintendent Fisher is. He'd chase us off.'

She considered me with concern, her head cocked. 'You worry me, Richard. It's not your usual attitude.'

I pursed my lips. 'Harry had it coming to him, as you must know, love. There'll be dozens of suspects. Husbands and men friends of some of the women Harry's accommodated—shall we say—in the past few years. It's the sort of thing the police can do—better than I could, anyway.'

'I just thought . . .' she began.

But I was ahead of her. 'Well . . . all right,' I agreed. 'We'll see what we can find out. Does that suit you, love?'

Amelia nodded, and smiled a thin smile. But I was still not optimistic about my chance of obtaining information. Of course, there was the old man on his bench to interview. He might have seen something relating to Harry's death. Might. But if so, he would be round at the police station, where they would be coaxing from him every last scrap of information he could supply. Anyway, it could be worth the journey, as long as Penny didn't turn up again, I thought grimly, with some new idea of discouraging me. She could not be very intelligent if she failed to realise that, by trying to steer me away from something which she might believe to be important, she was only sparking my interest in it.

So, after breakfast the following morning, and after I'd taken the dogs for our morning constitutional, we prepared to depart. I would have liked to use my Triumph Stag, as it hadn't had an outing for ages, but it's an open two-seater, which made it unsafe for the dogs, and they'd have gone berserk if we had left them behind. So it had to be Amelia's car, and this time she insisted on driving it herself.

'Can you remember the route?' I asked her.

'I expect so. But with you beside me, Richard, I can't go wrong.' She was using her solemn, teasing voice.

'Hah!' I said, and she stole a second from her concentration in order to glance at me. 'You'll remember it better than I could,' I told her.

She was silent until we drew close to our objective. The island. I remembered it.

'Straight on?' she asked.

'Straight on,' I agreed. 'And left at the traffic lights.'

No difficulties at all, it seemed. Very soon, we were climbing the hill called The Rock, but this time, at the top of it, we turned right, and could therefore park on the patch beyond the paddling pool.

As soon as I got out, and was on my feet, I could see that the bench was unoccupied. Of course, there was the likelihood that they still had the old chap round at the police station, but it was well past breakfast time, and I would have expected him to have been taken home long before this.

All right—so that was where he probably was. His real home. A roof over his head.

'Do you really need to see him?' Amelia asked, as I hadn't mentioned any aspects about which I might question him.

I shrugged. The hope was that he had seen something relating to the killing of Harry Martin, but one had to take into consideration the fact that he had a tendency to doze off. And in any event, the police would have drained him of any information relating to periods when he had been awake. Perhaps, then, the old man, sent home tired and full of police breakfast, and maybe the bun the uniformed woman sergeant had promised him, had retired to his bed in order to catch up with his sleeping, as opposed to napping, and do a bit of digesting.

It seemed that our trip was going to be abortive. But we could not simply turn away and drive home again without checking. From what the old man had said, he lived behind the fire station, which was visible just down a side street off the main road to Shropshire, a splash of red in an otherwise uninspiring street.

'I think I ought to *try* to see him,' I said. Then, at least we could leave the district, and go home with an easy conscience. I would have done all that was possible.

So . . . it was one dog lead each for Amelia and me, and the traffic lights to see us safely to the other side. One more minor road to cross, and the fire station was only a hundred yards away.

I had to suppose that the access to any dwellings at the rear was via the large area of concrete surface beside the station. It was a matter of walking round huge, but shallow pools of water. Perhaps it was necessary, every morning, to try out each hosepipe, ensuring it was clear. A bit like clearing one's throat, I thought. We picked our way round to the rear, and even though there seemed to be a routine check of equipment going on, nobody challenged us.

At the rear, there were large drains. The firefighters certainly used a lot of water to practise with. Keeping their eye in. And against a far wall were four dwellings, or sheds, or whatever you decided to describe them as. They reminded me of wartime pre-fabs. All four buildings were mostly of corrugated iron, which could be very cold in the winter, though one had to assume that they contained all the basic amenities and that a certain amount of insulation had been provided. Perhaps the fire service used them as rest-houses for the teams on duty. Only one had a name. The others were completely unmarked, but I found the named one at the far end of the row. All were very clean. With all the hose-testing going on, it would be a little tricky finding an opportunity to open your windows.

Only one had curtains, and those were somewhat tatty. This was also the only one named. Nirvana. It was painted on a board by an amateur with a very worn brush and an unsteady hand.

But before we had time to investigate whether the old man was home, there was a shout from behind us. 'What the hell d'you want?'

We turned. He was a large man in what I took to be off-duty clothes, though he was wearing rubber boots.

'Looking for somebody,' I told him.

'Who? What's his name?'

But of course I didn't know his name. 'I don't know,' I admitted. 'He usually sits on a bench by the paddling pool.'

'Oh . . . that'll be old Charlie. Ex-Chief Fire Officer.'

He was still uncertain about us. But the dogs hadn't growled. They detected no threat.

'He said something about living here,' I said.

'And so he does. What's your business with him? I'm not having you worrying him. Old Charlie's a living legend.'

I wondered whether there could be any psychological connection involved, to explain why an ex-fireman should daily sit beside a paddling pool, even though it was drained. Nostalgia? Or, perhaps, a strong desire to grab a hose and fill it up? There would be hydrant outlets all round the pool, I guessed.

'It's not a matter of worrying him,' I said. 'It's that I'm worrying about him. Why isn't he sitting on his bench by the paddling pool? It's a decent morning. Quite mild.'

'Isn't he?' He frowned heavily.

'No. We've just come from there.'

And at last he seemed to be concerned, and crossed to the end window of Nirvana, trying to peer inside.

'Can't see him,' he said. 'Let's just try the latch.'

There was no key-hole in the door, only a one-inch round hole through which, presumably, one put a finger in order to lift the latch inside. No security at all. But, judging by the alacrity with which this fire officer had appeared, there could be no concern about prowlers breaking and entering. And now, his finger probing through the hole, he lifted the latch on the other side and pushed open the door. Then he led the way inside. Amelia hesitated behind me. The dogs growled, way down in the back of their throats, and the fire officer stopped dead, blocking the doorway.

'Bloody hell!' he said, and he stepped back a pace.

I peered beyond his shoulder, then I reached for Amelia's arm. 'No, love,' I said. 'Better wait outside.' There was something wrong with my voice; my throat was dry.

'Richard!'

'Please,' I said. 'You don't want to see this.'

Her eyes were suddenly wide and startled, and her hand flew to her mouth.

181

Old Charlie, as the fireman had called him, was on his knees beside his bed, as though praying. He had fallen like that, his head sideways on the duvet, which had absorbed a considerable amount of blood. One blow, it seemed, had not been considered sufficient, and his killer had made certain with one or two more, though any one of them would have been enough. It bore the mark of a panic assault.

'Let's get out of here,' said the fireman, his voice uncertain, though his working life must have included sights much more appalling.

But this was personal, the death of a friend and colleague, a violent death.

'I've got to get to a phone,' he said, choking on the words. 'Can you—'

'I'll guard it,' I said. 'I'm ex-police. And ask for Superintendent Fisher.'

'Why him?'

'You must have heard. A violent death by the paddling pool . . . this could be linked with it.'

But he looked blank. His duties probably absorbed all his time.

'A man named Martin was killed by the paddling pool, the night before last,' I told him, now including more detail, but not including what seemed obvious to me—the motive for this vicious killing. It had been assumed that Charlie could have observed the assault on Harry Martin.

'Yeah?' he said. 'Well . . . we've got our own troubles to look after. But I'll ask for that superintendent. What was the name, again?'

'Fisher.'

'Right. Shall I tell him—'

'Tell him there's another death, and that'll do. He'll be here before you can hang up.'

'Right. Shall I tell him—'

'Just tell him there's another death, and where, and that'll do.' He was obviously finding it hard to take anything in.

'Yeah,' he said. 'Right.' He looked around him, still somewhat dazed, his reactions in a tangle.

But he seemed to be emotionally unaffected by the old man's death, perhaps not really accepting it, the shock holding back the impact until later, whereas inside I was raging. I wanted something I could kick in fury, or someone's face, which I could not see in my mind with any clarity, but which I could punch until it was completely unrecognisable. Amelia jerked at my arm.

'Richard . . .'

I turned her away, taking her arm. 'You don't want to see.'

She grimaced. 'It's him? The old man . . .' Her voice slid away.

'Yes. And he's dead.'

'You're quite sure?' she whispered.

'I'm quite sure.'

She covered her face with her hands.

183

Nobody could have lived with the injuries that had been inflicted. The attack had been frenetic; the duvet was soaked with blood.

Charlie was in his pyjamas, which were also soaked with his own blood, and he had obviously put up something of a fight, even at his age. I thought his right forearm lay at an awkward angle. It was probably broken.

There could have been no necessity for what seemed to have been an onslaught of rage. Rage that Charlie had not died at the first blow; that he had put up a defence? A rage of fear, that he might have found the ability to fight back?

I turned. 'Don't come in . . .'

But Amelia had left me. I followed her away from the sheds, and together we waited for Superintendent Fisher. There was nothing to say. What we shared could not be expressed in words. Her hand, clutching my arm, was shaking.

Then he was back, the fireman. 'He's on his way,' he said.

'You mean Fisher? Did you get the right man?'

'Yes.'

'Did he say anything?'

'Yes. But I can't repeat it, in front of your wife.' And the fireman drifted away again.

I glanced at Amelia. She was sobbing into one of those scraps of linen that women call handkerchiefs. 'Why?' she whispered.

'He could have seen something that would have been dangerous to whoever it was.'

'Harry?' she suggested. 'Harry's death?'

'That—or something like it. But the pity, the real and genuine pity of it, is that he's been at the police station, handing out every last detail of what he might have seen, and he was killed unnecessarily. He had already unloaded all he knew. But this murdering bastard couldn't have known that.'

'Yes,' she said. 'Yes, Richard.'

There was then silence between us, as we waited for Fisher to arrive. I was tensed, poised for action in a way I could not visualise.

I had seen other horrible deaths; mangled remains after car crashes, of what had been human beings. But there was something different about this old man's death, a decisive disposal of a human being who would have been incapable of harming anyone, and whose only fault had been in being there—sitting on a bench from which he might, or might not, have witnessed the death of Harry Martin. But that, surely, could not have been the sole reason for such a violent and repulsive attack. That he *might* have seen something. Might. And he had, in any event, been in the habit of dozing off. Anything happening that was vitally important could well have been during one of his naps.

It was the suggestion that he had been disposed of simply because of a vague possibility which so infuriated me. I wanted him, this murderer. Wanted my hands on him. I was aching with the desire to beat him until I was too close to exhaustion to continue.

'Richard . . .' Amelia was tugging at my sleeve. 'Richard . . . please . . .'

I turned my head, and stared at her. For a moment I felt disorientated. Amelia had ceased to exist. My mind was fighting to be free of this overpowering fury, and my vision was blurred.

'Sorry, love.' I struggled with my emotions. 'Sorry—my mind was elsewhere.'

She was staring into my face with concern. 'I thought . . .' she said, a catch in her voice, 'I thought for a moment that you were quite insane.'

And so I had been, I had to agree. For just a few moments. The death of this man, who, in his working life, must have saved the lives of a considerable number of people, was something I could not easily assimilate. The fact that whoever had done this was alive, and walking free, was completely unacceptable . . . Then there was the tugging at my sleeve again. Amelia—attracting my attention. I looked down into her face, harried now, her cheeks white and drawn.

'No, Richard,' she whispered. 'Please . . . no.'

'No what?' I asked. It did not sound like my voice, not from my side of it.

'No to what you intend,' she whispered, raising herself on to her toes and kissing me on the cheek.

'How do you know what I intend, my love? I'm not sure, myself.'

'I know you.' She nodded decisively. 'Now it means I'll have to hang on your arm, and make sure you behave like a normal human being.'

'I *am* a normal—'

But she cut in briskly. 'Not now. At this moment, you are not, Richard. If you could see your face in a mirror . . . Have I got to hang on your arm every minute, to make sure that when you face him—and you *will* face him, I know that—whatever it takes, you'll face him . . . But I'll not have you descending to the depths of a wild and vicious animal.'

'Amelia—'

'To the depths of the person who did this.'

'Amelia —'

'Promise me, Richard.'

'How can I—'

'You're capable of it, I know,' she went on, taking my hand in hers, and pressing the back of it to her cheek. 'And whatever you did— however violent—I could understand. But Richard, love, you'd be lowering yourself to the level of this beast who's . . . who's . . .' Then she realised that she'd already said the same thing.

She could not continue with it, emotion suddenly taking control. After a few moments, while I clasped her closely to me, she raised her head.

'Promise me, Richard,' she whispered.

I hate being forced into promises. 'Promise what?' I asked warily, though I knew very well what she meant.

'That when you find him—and you will, Richard love, you will—when you put a hand on him it'll be to arrest him—and no more.'

When I was aching to get my hands on him and tear him apart, that was what she asked! It was unfair, trapping me with her own emotional response.

'Richard?' she whispered.

I sighed. 'All right. I promise.'

But heavens, could I keep it?

Then Fisher was at my elbow. I had heard no police siren, caught no glimpse of a flashing beacon.

'Which one is it?' he demanded, and I pointed, still somewhat stunned, to Nirvana.

I spoke quietly to Amelia. 'Let's get away from here, love.'

'Yes,' she whispered. 'Away.'

We walked back towards the paddling pool, slowly, not speaking. The dogs had detected the mood, and seemed unhappy.

Without any consultation, we crossed at the pedestrian crossing, and went straight to the bench. Our friend Charlie's bench. There, we sat. I had a vague idea that it would be as well to stay around for a while, in case Fisher wanted to speak to us—to ask us questions. I was also fully aware that it would be some while before either Amelia or I would be able to drive safely. The dogs were restless, and thrust their squat faces at us, on my lap and on Amelia's. They had to be reassured that there was nothing about their behaviour that had upset us.

They could not be expected to understand that this situation had become something very personal to me. Sometime in the future, I knew, I would find myself face to face with the person who had killed the old man. I would then take decisive and violent action. And if the dogs were present, they would come to my assistance, and somebody, whom I could not yet place in my mind, would be considerably mauled. And from that would develop an opinion, from some idiot or other, that the dogs were savage and beyond control, and that they should be put down. Over my dead body, I thought, when I should have been thinking about someone else's dead body. The old man's.

But again—and this, had been so since this whole business had begun—there was no evidence that I could perceive, nothing at all in the way of clues. No cigarette stub on the floor, either stamped out or pinched out, in Connie's style. No footprint impressed on any surface, as all the surfaces were concrete. No dropped handkerchief that I might remember somebody using. And . . . this being the critical consideration . . . no possible weapon left behind. Or at least, not one that in any way matched the contusions.

Yet this fact was, in itself, a clue, or at least an indicator. With Harry's death, there had been no weapon left behind, and now the same applied to old Charlie's death. With cold determination, I set my mind to scouring the most unpleasant facts relating to the two killings, first of Harry Martin, and now of Charlie. The contusions to the head were very much alike, though poor Charlie's wounds were distributed to other vulnerable parts of the body. But Charlie had put up a fight. Harry, attacked from behind, had had no chance. One single blow would have been sufficient. And if the same weapon had been used, and as no such weapon had been visible in the old man's room, then it meant that it was being carried around, as a policeman might carry his truncheon. Or possibly, taken away, and discarded somewhere, where it might never be found.

There had seemed to be no point in staying at the fire station. Both Amelia and I had sensed that we would feel much better elsewhere. And what more logical, and in fact symbolic, than that we should have returned to Charlie's bench seat. But there was nothing significant to be seen here either: grass and the trees around the pool, the main road beyond, and the shops beyond the road.

I knew exactly where Harry had died. There, in fact, was the spread of scattered brown leaves, as the police had left them. Since that time there had been no wind. In fact, the very stillness of the fallen leaves, and of the leaves remaining on the trees, was soporific. I very nearly dozed off myself, and I knew, then, how easy and inevitable it had been for old Charlie to have relaxed into one of his little naps.

Yet something seemed out of place in the scene. For a minute or two I tried to capture this furtive thought as it slipped across my mind. Then I realised what it was. Due to the positioning of the trees—a purely haphazard arrangement—it was not possible from this bench to see the spot where Harry had been struck down. The trunks of three trees, one close to us and two further away, seemed to overlap. I tried moving from one end of the bench to the other, having to suffer—and trying to ignore—various remarks from Amelia as to my sanity.

But from no position on the bench could I see the exact spot where Harry had been struck down and fallen into the paddling pool. It followed, therefore, that from where Harry had died it would not have been possible to see the old man on this bench.

And it followed from this that it would not have been possible for Harry's assailant to have realised that anyone was sitting on that bench, until he—or she, I had to suppose— moved away from the scene of Harry's death. It had been a pure supposition, then, that old Charlie had witnessed the murder of Harry.

And all I was doing, therefore, was to think myself even deeper into the realisation that Charlie's death had been the meaningless destruction of a life, which infuriated me even more than I had been before. Useless, stupid . . . and appalling, that was what it had been.

CHAPTER ELEVEN

I dreamt, that night, of an empty room. No doors, no windows, no furniture, no anything. In it, I was trapped, but I knew that there *was* a way out. There had to be, and I could not locate it. I awoke with a start, and Amelia was saying, 'Richard, Richard . . .'

'Ummh?' I said.

'You were talking to yourself. In your sleep.'

'Sorry, love. I woke you, did I?'

'Of course. You kept calling my name. Then I opened the door for you. It was what you asked.'

'Umm? And what was on the other side?'

'I don't know. It was your dream, not mine.'

Then we slept again, and my dream did not return. Over breakfast, Amelia said, 'You were having a nightmare, Richard.'

'Was I?'

'Something about a room.'

'Umm. I don't remember any of it,' I said. 'The dream—I can't remember.'

'Well . . .' She smiled. 'It doesn't really matter, does it?'

'I suppose not.'

Nevertheless, I felt that it did. If it had not been important I would not have dreamt it.

But I knew that this was fallacious. Dreams were always only vaguely linked with reality.

And yet . . . no room into which I could remember walking had been empty. Sylvia Thomas's kitchen—on that night of the storm—had contained her dead body. The room had been empty only of her life. And the room, the home, where Charlie had lived— that had contained Charlie's dead body. But Harry—ah yes, Harry had not died in a room. He had been standing at the edge of the paddling pool . . . waiting. So there *had* been a valid phone call. 'I'll meet you at the pool.' Something like that. And at ten o'clock, with only the street lights dimly filtering through the trees, anyone—anyone at all—could have been lurking in the shadows. Someone carrying a weapon, it had to be, because the wound to the crown of Harry's head had been repeated with Charlie as the victim. The same weapon, it seemed to me. The same target . . . the crown of the head.

But I was getting nowhere with these wandering thoughts. Not a clue anywhere, except that blasted wrist-watch with the thumbprint on its glass. That had been a different setting, a different crime, a different weapon.

'Are you intending to go there again, today?' Amelia asked, the table now cleared and only the breakfast washing-up to be completed.

'I thought we might.'

'But for what?' she asked. 'I can't think of anything we have to do, or even need to.'

'Just sit on the bench,' I admitted. 'Sit and think.'

'And a lot of good *that* will do,' she said dismissively.

I shrugged. 'I'd just like to *be* there. Something might turn up.'

She gave me a very thin smile. 'I can't wait. It all sounds so exciting!' Then she grimaced at me ruefully.

'I'll take the dogs out,' I said.

'Yes, do that,' Amelia agreed, her tone suggesting that she would be glad to see the back of me for a while.

I don't think I said a word to the dogs, just let them run wild. But, in a way secret to themselves, they discovered that something was worrying me, and they failed to play me up, as they normally did. We went our usual walk as far as the derelict farmhouse, the dogs indulged in their usual exploration through the remaining sections of walls, and then we walked back.

It suddenly occurred to me that we hadn't seen the woman police sergeant at all, the previous day. Perhaps her duties had not allowed her the spare time. I wondered whether she had heard about Charlie's death. I wondered what she felt about it, if she had. And now I couldn't wait to get going. I knew I had one person, apart from Amelia, who would feel exactly as I did about Charlie's death, and who would be equally anxious to uncover the killer.

We left home a little after ten o'clock, Amelia, the two dogs, and me. I was driving. Very little was said on the trip. Nothing was discussed.

When I turned in, opposite the clock, I noticed that it was still showing exactly the same time as the day before. Did they ever wind it? I wondered. Better no clock at all than a stopped one. But I had spared a moment in which to catch one glimpse of Charlie's bench seat. A woman was sitting there—not in uniform. But I could detect, even in the second that the glimpse allowed, that she was Charlie's woman sergeant.

We parked, and I released the dogs as soon as I'd slammed the doors. At once they ran for Charlie's bench seat. Whether they believed that Charlie would be there, or whether they, too, had spotted that Charlie's bench now had another friend as its occupant, I couldn't tell. In any event, she had warning of our approach. She looked round, and managed a grimace that might have been a welcoming smile, if stress had not distorted it.

'You know?' she asked, her voice flat and tired. 'About Charlie . . .'

'Yes,' I said. 'I was the one who found him.'

Amelia and I then took our seats, each side of her.

'Anything?' I asked.

She knew at once what I meant. 'Nothing,'

she said. 'Absolutely no lead or clue. There's nothing to go on.' She sounded dull and emotionless.

'Umm!' I said. Then we all three sat silent, and stared at the empty pool. The dogs were searching the territory immediately around us.

After at least five minutes of silence, during which a feeling of useless contemplation captured us, our sergeant friend spoke up, apparently merely to bring some life into our meeting.

'You'll be here for the show?' she asked.

'Show?' asked Amelia. 'What show?'

'Tomorrow evening.' The sergeant was desperately attempting to drag her mind—and ours, I felt—from the death of Charlie. 'It'll be the fifth of November. Bonfire night,' she explained.

I had given no thought to that fact. Since my teens had been left behind, bonfire night had ceased to attract my attention.

'What about bonfire night?' I asked.

'It's the show the fire brigade puts on, around the pool.'

As I had always assumed that the firemen were very busy on bonfire night, putting out fires that had run amok, I had difficulty in imagining them finding any spare time for letting off their own bangers and rockets, and dancing around their own bonfire. If that was what they did . . . before putting it out with their multiple hoses, of course.

'Do they have their own bonfire?' I asked tentatively.

It seemed rather unlikely, with all the trees that were around the paddling pool, which, now being dry, was the only practical venue in that area for a bonfire.

'Not a bonfire, surely?' I asked again, as she seemed not to have been listening.

When she responded, there was a lighter tone to her voice. She was desperately attempting to detach her thoughts from Charlie's death.

'No,' she said. 'Not a bonfire. The opposite, rather.' She managed a thin smile.

I used up a few seconds in order to wonder how one could have the opposite to a bonfire.

'I don't understand,' I had to admit.

'It's a water show,' she said, as though that made everything clear. Which it didn't. When I glanced at her, I saw that she was amused at my reaction.

'What on earth's a water show?' I asked.

She had been poised, waiting for that question. Now she produced the answer, though her voice once more contained the dead tone that I thought she had managed to cast away.

'It'll be a special show. It always is,' she said, brightening a little and with obvious pride, as though it was hers. 'Tomorrow evening, at about eight. You mustn't miss it. It was Charlie's idea, in the first place, when he was

Chief Fire Officer. "Something different," he said. "Something safer." I think he had the idea that he might attract a lot of people away from lighting their own bonfires, which so often got out of control. Eight or nine years ago, that was, when he thought of it. Mind you, it didn't work out quite as he'd hoped. It didn't help much, you see, when it came to it. The emergency calls still came in to their station, though each year the crowd's grown larger around the pool, to watch Charlie's water show. But even so, he still had to send up a few rockets, otherwise people would reckon they'd been cheated. So he tried sending up rockets through the spray, and it worked all right. It's become a very popular part of the show. You must come—you really can't afford to miss it.'

She was silent. I glanced at Amelia, who simply gave me an empty smile, and raised her eyebrows.

'We'll be here,' I promised. 'I'm not sure about the dogs, though.'

We could, of course, leave them at home with Mary, but experience indicated that, though they did not actually pine, they would pester Mary, every second of our absence, to take them out or to produce Amelia and me by some magic means.

'Oh . . .' said our new friend, 'you needn't worry about bringing the dogs. No bangers. Nothing, really, to upset them.'

'Umm!' I said dubiously, glancing at

Amelia, who seemed equally unconvinced.

'We'll certainly come, if things are all right,' I told the sergeant. 'At home, I mean. Eight o'clock, did you say?'

'Around that time.'

'But what, exactly, happens?' I asked, as she hadn't explained.

'Oh . . . didn't I say? No, of course I didn't. It's just that the firemen . . . they like to get ten men on the job, as there're ten hydrants, though I don't suppose they need to be genuine firemen. Anybody could do it.' She smiled at us, probably at our blank expressions. 'I'm not explaining this very well, am I?'

I returned her smile, and shook my head. 'I'm afraid it's not very clear, yet,' I told her.

'Sorry. I'll have another go at it. They have a fireman at each of the ten hydrants round the pool, and they attach their hoses. Adjustable, they are, from a strong jet to a fine spray. They put them all on "spray", and point them up and over the pool, overlapping, sort of, and they shine different colours of lights through it, and get lovely effects.'

I looked at Amelia, who raised her eyebrows at me. What . . . no bangers? No bonfire?

'Sort of *l'eau et lumière,*' I suggested.

The sergeant raised her eyebrows at me. 'If you want to give it fancy names, that about covers it. And they *do* fire away rockets, right

200

through the centre of the spray. It's really worth watching. But you'd better bring macs or something. Slickers, say. Umbrellas would get in your way, looking up.'

'Yes,' said Amelia. 'We've already got our waterproof stuff, in the car.'

'So I'll see you then,' said the sergeant getting to her feet. 'Tomorrow, about eight o'clock. And now . . . I'd better get back to the station. I'm supposed to be on duty.'

We watched her leave. Amelia said, 'Do you think it would be worth the trip, Richard?'

'You mean the show?' I asked. 'Oh, I think so, judging by what she's told us. It's rather intriguing, as a matter of fact. And in any event, we've promised.'

'But . . . what about the dogs?' Amelia was still concerned about Sheba and Jake.

I gave it a few seconds of consideration. 'I can't think that it would upset them,' I decided. 'If they get a bit of spray on them, they'll think it's raining, and *that* never worries them. It's bangers that they wouldn't like.'

'Umm!' she said, nodding in agreement. The sergeant had said there would be no bangers.

So we returned home, and decided what would be the best to take as practical waterproofs, as our umbrellas might prove to be cumbersome, it seemed.

By seven o'clock the following evening we were ready to leave. As I would be doing the driving, I was giving myself plenty of time for the trip. Parking would no doubt be difficult. The sky was clear and there was no suggestion of rain in the weather forecast. Not, it would seem, from what we had already been told, that rain would make any difference.

I drove straight there, with no pause for thought, now that I knew every yard of the journey.

I tried the tarmac parking patch first, but it was already packed with cars, so I stopped, got out, and looked around. Beyond that scrappy line of hedges was the extensive area of grassland, about which I already knew. This was also now in use as a parking area. Whether it was authorised or not, I did not consider for more than a few seconds, but got back behind the wheel and edged our way through the widest of the gaps in the hedgerow, as tyre tracks indicated that I would not be alone. Which proved to be true. It seemed that the show had certainly achieved a reputation. Even there, I had to look around before I could locate a parking space, and this was beside a black Volkswagen Beetle, from which Connie was at that moment alighting. She directed us in. After all, she wouldn't want any dents or scratches on her precious old Beetle.

We all got out, the dogs recognising a friend. Connie crouched down and fussed them. She hadn't brought her own puppies, I noticed. Perhaps it was as well.

This, being grassland, was rather mushy. I looked around. There was not much to see except the vague shapes of the parked cars. No sign of Philip's motor cycle, as far as I could see.

'He's found somewhere else to leave it, then,' I said to Connie, as Philip could possibly have found a corner for the Suzuki on the tarmac surface of the proper car-park.

'Who are you talking about?' asked Connie, hunting for her waterproofs in the boot.

'Well . . . Philip. I was making the point that of course he wouldn't need to lean his bike against your car, this time. Not with a solid tarmac footing available. Whereas . . . that awful evening of the storm when Sylvia Thomas died, he had to lean the bike he had at that time against your passenger's door. Did much damage, did it? It sounded like it, the way he put it. Brake lever sliding down your door. Passenger side,' I repeated, as she was staring at me blankly.

'What on earth are you talking about?' she asked, still baffled.

'That night . . . the night of Sylvia Thomas's death.'

'For heaven's sake, that was ten years ago . . . and don't I know it! What does it matter, now? Let's get to the pool. They'll be starting any minute.'

'Do you mean,' I persisted, reaching for her arm to detain her, 'that you don't remember that terrible evening? The night Sylvia Thomas died?'

'Of course I remember.' She shook her arm free. 'Why are we talking about it now? Wasting time.'

'I was just asking, Connie, in a friendly sort of way, how you got on with the scratching down your passenger door. No sign of it now—none that I can see. They did a good job of it. Or did you have to pay for a new door?'

'Oh . . . come *on*. We'll miss the beginning. There weren't any scratches and I don't know what you're talking about.'

I glanced at Amelia. As far as I could tell, in the poor light, she was frowning.

'Philip told me,' I said to Connie, 'that he leaned his motor bike against your Beetle's passenger door, and when you drove away it slid off, scratching it.'

'Nonsense,' she said. 'Let's get moving. I don't want to miss a second of it.'

Then she walked away briskly, and inside twenty yards she had disappeared from my sight, leaving me to consider the implication in her statement. If Philip had not—as he had claimed—leaned his motor bike against the Volks, then against what had he leaned it? He, himself, had told me that he hadn't been able to use the prop-stand at all, as it had sunk into the mud when he tried it.

But I jolted my mind from the past, as we were not quite ready to face the present. We

204

had to attach the dogs' leads and put on our slickers and waterproof hats. Then we took an umbrella each, just in case, and headed for the pool. It was five minutes to eight, and when we had edged our way through the shrubbery I saw that the grassland surrounding the pool was packed almost solid, shoulder to shoulder, with spectators. The sergeant had been quite correct when she had boasted about the popularity of the show. Across the main road, the clock in the tower was showing the correct time. Not only that—the two dials that I could see at an angle were illuminated. I had to assume that the other two were, as well. Festival indeed!

Abruptly, seeming to have come out of nowhere, our sergeant was beside us, and Penny had emerged from the throng to hover at my other shoulder.

'They'll be starting any minute, now,' said the sergeant. I tightened my grip on the dogs' leads, as she moved away.

Then lights were switched on. Coloured spotlights, fastened in the trees surrounding us, were linked by electric cables stretching through the tree branches, and with their multi-coloured rays aimed across and down at the empty pool.

There was a strange silence, as though hundreds of spectators were all holding their breaths at the same time.

Suddenly, at a shout of 'Let's go!', ten hoses

in ten expert pairs of hands, distributed around the pool, were turned on; they were adjusted to 'fine spray', and were being waved around erratically, but clearly with the intention that the water should fall into the pool. It seemed, almost, that the spray bit into the rays of coloured light, as it tossed the colours around, from shimmering to penetrating, and wrapped in sudden bursts of rainbow arcs.

'Isn't it splendid?' said Amelia, hugging my arm.

But the man who had initiated this display was no longer sitting on his bench seat, and enjoying it all. At this thought, I said to Penny, 'He's dead, you know.'

'What!' She clutched at my arm. 'Who?' She shook it. 'Who's dead?'

'Charlie. The man who thought this up. Invented it. Dead.'

'Oh,' she said. 'What a pity he's missing it. You gave me quite a turn, then.'

'Sorry,' I said.

I could not think of anything more to say on this subject, and looked away from her. Approaching us again was the sergeant, I realised, though it seemed to me that she was not enjoying this evening. Charlie's death was probably intruding into her pleasure, although I had the impression that her actions at this time were imposed on her. Superintendent Fisher was behind her. I suddenly noticed that

Penny had disappeared.

'Isn't it marvellous!' the sergeant called out, when she was close enough for her raised voice to cut through what was now a considerable din. Uncoordinated cheers, and shouts of pleasure, competed with the penetrating hiss and thrum of the hoses. From time to time, the hose operators switched from spray to jet, almost vertically and possibly for the fun of it. Suddenly, umbrellas blossomed, to be used more as defensive equipment from the jets than protection from the spray. The water thundered against the umbrellas. Shrieks of exaggerated dismay pierced the accumulating noise, and the umbrellas were being waved around as the water assault varied in accordance with the whims of the hose-handlers.

'Let's get away from here,' I said to Amelia, but she responded by gripping my arm.

'No, Richard! It's fun . . . fun . . .'

But it was clearly not fun for Fisher. He was approaching us now, with Penny's arm gripped in his large and practised hand, and with an extensive scowl twisting his face.

'The man's insane!' Penny screamed, only a piercing scream being capable now of cutting through the almost-solid impact of the tangled and rain-soaked blare of noise.

'What's this?' I asked, as they joined us.

Fisher did not release Penny's arm. Behind him and around him, like shadows and reflections of glittering, rain-sodden rags, was

207

a group of five men, in anoraks and floppy yellow hats, water streaming down their faces, grim now, unrelenting. Not one of them had come to enjoy the show, and their scowls underlined it.

'They've taken him away!' Penny screamed.

Fisher stopped, half raising his spare arm to halt his small squad.

'Taken who away?' I asked him, as he released Penny's arm. She ran at once to me.

'Keep out of this, Patton,' Fisher demanded.

'I *am* out of it. Who have you taken away, as the young lady claims? It's not a secret, is it?'

'His name's Philip Martin.'

'You've taken *him* away?' I persisted. 'Philip Martin? Then you've got it all wrong, Superintendent. All wrong.'

'Oh God!' he said. 'Here we go again. Can't you keep your damned opinions to yourself, Patton?'

With a certain amount of dignity, as I felt that Amelia was giggling at my elbow, I said, 'I'm naturally interested. If you've got a valid reason for arresting him—'

'Not arrested,' he said, his voice approaching a tone that resembled a growl. 'For interrogation.'

I shrugged. 'There's nothing he could tell you, and it still rates as detention.'

'We'll see, won't we!'

'Nothing that I couldn't help you with, myself,' I explained. 'Why take him away? You

208

might, at least, have let him watch the show.'

'The show!' he said with disgust. 'Some people never grow up.'

'Perhaps we ought to envy them.' I was having to raise my voice almost to a shout, for the combined verbal applause from the crowd and the hiss and thrum of the water, which seemed to be growing in volume, had reduced him to a mere mask of moving lips, which had to be read rather than listened to.

He released the force of his grip on Penny's arm, and she snatched it free. Automatically, it seemed, as she turned to me. Perhaps she saw in me a haven of sense and logic. I hoped she did.

'They've locked him away!' she shouted. Water dripped from her chin.

'And we know,' I said to her, 'you and I— even if our clever superintendent thinks he's got the right man by arresting Philip Martin— *we* know otherwise, don't we, Penny? We know he's wrong. Here, let me have that shoulder bag. It's obviously too heavy for you to carry around. What've you got in there? Philip's tools for his bike?'

'Yes. That's what's in here.'

'Let me,' I offered, stretching out my right hand. 'I'll keep it safe for him.'

'No!' She turned away, half a rotation, so that the shoulder bag now lay on the hip away from me, as though she treasured it. But of course she would; it belonged to Philip.

A rocket, displaced from its intended route, zipped past our heads, with barely a yard of clearance. Penny screamed, ducking her head, and Amelia gripped my arm even more tightly. Sheba howled, and Jake growled, way down in his throat. I began to think it had not been a good idea to bring them. The rockets were now being let off in large numbers, and spray from all directions caught them as they rose into the air. Screams of delight echoed around us as bursts of coloured stars exploded in the sky.

Our tight group seemed to have grown, with reserve officers, and they surrounded us as though protecting us from the possible danger of the rockets. These hissed through the pall of spray, and roared upwards. There was now about a foot of water in the pool.

'We can't stay here, Richard,' said Amelia. 'The dogs don't like it at all. I think they're going to start panicking soon.'

Jake and Sheba had set back their heads and were howling together mournfully. Amelia crouched down, and flung an arm around each neck. She was rewarded by having the water cleared from her face, a large tongue to each cheek. Then she looked up at me. 'I think I've had enough of this, Richard,' she admitted. 'Can't we leave now?'

But our group was closing around us, and quite tightly, as though we were precious. To be protected. Or was it: to be restrained? In any event, the major part of the group being large police constables, they offered a certain physical amount of protection from the water. Amelia, without having to crouch, stood no higher than any of the shoulders around us, · and Penny was barely two inches taller than Amelia.

'At least,' I said to Penny, bending towards her ear, 'Philip didn't have to worry about parking the Suzuki against Connie's Beetle. Not this time.'

'I don't know what you mean,' shouted Penny.

'You're not the only one,' said Fisher, who didn't need to raise his voice, because it was normally forceful and penetrating.

'I wouldn't expect you to know, Super,' I said to him. 'It's to do with a murder ten years or so ago. Near to Bridgnorth. A woman was killed in her own house. She was a prostitute. Not a street-walking prostitute, but a little more classy than that. She would have preferred to be called a mistress. It sounds better, and probably costs more. The weather at that time was terrible. Pouring rain, pitch darkness, and nothing but mud to be encountered in all directions. Harry Martin was one of that lady's clients—and his son hated it. As did the son's girlfriend. You have the son, Philip Martin, in custody. This young lady here, Penny Downes, was—and still is—Philip's girlfriend. And, that night, the mistress, Sylvia Thomas, was killed with a rolling-pin, which just happened to be on the kitchen table. We thought this had been done by Connie Martin, Harry Martin's widow now, and she went to prison for it. I believe—'

'Can't you cut it short?' Fisher demanded.

'This *is* the shortened version,' I assured him. 'I intended to say that I now believe that Sylvia Thomas, the mistress, was not killed by Connie Martin. My principal reason for arresting Connie was simply because she was there, and she had a good motive. The weather, that evening, was so very bad that the house, where Sylvia Thomas was killed, was almost isolated by the River Severn, at the rear, and a vast expanse of mud at the front. Connie said that she had not actually stopped her car, but had turned away while her tyres still had a bit of grip left. I didn't believe her at the time, and charged her with the murder of her husband's mistress. Now she's free, and I believe I'm very close to being able to prove that she did not kill Sylvia Thomas after all.'

'Oh . . . come on,' he said impatiently. 'Cut it short. We're standing here, getting wet through, and you're burbling on and on.'

I was aware that Amelia was still at my shoulder, and now Penny closed up on my other side. Philip was not there to protect her, but I was quite certain she could protect herself, and didn't need any assistance from me.

'Don't you ever think in terms of motivations?' I asked Fisher. 'Why . . . why . . . why. Damn it, that can be the most important aspect.'

'I'm not interested,' he said flatly. 'It's facts that matter.'

'Then you ought to be interested,' I told him impatiently. 'What happened ten years ago, at Bridgnorth, could be the motivation for what's happening now.'

'Nonsense. They're going mad with those hoses. Did you see that!'

Rockets were still whooshing up into the sky. Amelia fumbled for my hand, and Penny shouted, 'Why don't you go and let him out? Philip's done nothing.'

'His father's dead,' Fisher snapped impatiently. 'I intend to charge him with that murder.'

'You're surely not saying . . .' I tried to put in. But the rest of my sentence was cut short by the explosion of an extra-loud rocket into a mass of golden lights. I tried again. 'You're surely not saying that Philip had anything at all to do with his father's death! Harry's.'

'I'm not saying anything,' Fisher said tersely. 'But you know damned well, Patton, that most murders happen within the family.'

'I know nothing of the sort,' I answered briskly.

'Inheritance. Who'll inherit Harry Martin's money? That's the point.'

'I haven't seen Philip jumping around with joy,' I told him. 'Oh . . . talk sense, Superintendent. Do you think that Harry Martin was rolling in money? Have you seen the transport he used? It's a clapped-out old Land Rover.'

'No, I haven't,' he snapped out, impatient with me now, and distracted by the continuing rockets, though they did, at last, seem to be easing off. 'No—and I don't want to see it.'

'That Land Rover,' I told him, 'was used by this young woman here, Penny Downes, to try to drive us off the road. She failed. Check with your central station.'

'I can't accept—'

'Then simply listen,' I said, raising my voice to shout down the continuing hiss and growl of a loose scattering of passing rockets. 'This young woman, here, was in the locality, ten years or so ago, when Harry Martin's mistress, living in a cottage near Bridgnorth, was killed. To this young woman . . .'

I paused. Penny was clutching at my arm. Her face was distorted with fear, but no longer fear of the rockets, rather in fear of the way the men around us were closing in. I had to raise my voice louder. Now the noise surrounding us had no connection with the passing rockets, which seemed to have become less frequent, less disturbing. It was now a growling rumble from the group of men. I tried to ignore their presence, and continued

214

with my charge.

'To this young woman,' I went on, linking up with what I'd been saying, 'Harry Martin, her boyfriend Philip's father, was a menace. He was at the site, that terrible evening, I believe, and he could have seen things that I never knew about. And didn't *he* die, with a blow to the crown of his head? Just like poor old Charlie.'

'Now listen here,' said Fisher, drawing up close to me, seeking for a contact more intimate, as the firefighters began to close in on us. This was of interest to them. Charlie's name had been mentioned.

'Now listen here,' Fisher repeated, as I was clearly not listening to him. 'Let's have all this round at the station. My office. More private.'

But I didn't want it more private. Penny was shrinking from the police group, from Fisher, but she was not appealing to me for help. No. I was suddenly the enemy. She actually stamped in anger. I hadn't seen that reaction for ages.

'Prove it, prove it,' she shouted into my face, and poor Amelia was at a loss as to how she should react.

'I can prove it,' I said, but to Fisher, assuring him that I was not merely playing with words and unsubstantiated charges.

'Going right back to the death of Sylvia Thomas—Harry's mistress,' I continued, turning to Fisher, 'I can substantiate it all. But perhaps it *would* be done better in your office.'

I looked round me at the ranks of set faces, a barrage of them. Charlie's old friends and colleagues. They expected to hear more about their idol's death.

'Say it now,' Fisher growled at me.

'All right. All right. Go back ten years. The death of Sylvia Thomas, Harry's mistress. A house. Barely any access to it, the river one side—the rear—and a vast expanse of mud the other. The death too of Charlie, I can explain. If you'll give me the time.'

I was aware that the hoses had abruptly ceased to hiss, that the fine spray clothing us was slowly dripping away. The firefighters were now all gathered around us. The rest of the crowd, sensing that the show was over for another year, began to drift off in the direction of the car-park.

'Charlie!' snapped Fisher. 'Let's hear about Charlie.'

'Well—obviously—Charlie must have been killed because he could have seen, from his favourite bench, the actual killing of Harry Martin. And Harry was killed because he knew too much about the death of Sylvia Thomas. She was, after all, his mistress. Harry was there, that terrible, black evening. He saw exactly what happened . . .'

I paused for thought. Had I any evidence that Harry *had* been there? 'His Land Rover was parked at the far side of an extensive area of plain, sloppy mud,' I said. 'He'd taken Sylvia a present—it was her birthday.'

'All right, all right,' cut in Fisher. 'Are you saying that Harry Martin killed that prostitute?'

'No. No, I'm not saying that.'

I felt myself to be under pressure. The firemen were straining to hear our every word, most of them still clutching their hoses—but with the water turned off at the nozzles. There was now more than a foot of water in the pool.

'Then what the hell *are* you saying?' Fisher said impatiently.

I sighed. It was going to be difficult to put across to him—to him, and to the firefighters around us, who were interested in hearing about Charlie, but nothing else. The background noise of the departing crowd was distracting.

'What I'm saying,' I went on steadily, 'is that Harry Martin was visiting his mistress, Sylvia Thomas. And those two—Penny Downes and her boyfriend, Philip Martin—were determined to visit her, to discourage her, to warn her off. They hated her.'

'Don't make a meal of it,' said Fisher grumpily. 'Just the facts.'

'All right,' I agreed. 'They'd have been using Philip's motor bike. I think the bike at that time was a Triumph three-fifty twin. A heavy bike. And what they had to contend with was a vast stretch of mud. There was nowhere to lean the bike, and the prop-stand would sink into the mud. It would be quite useless. There'd be only one thing to do, in order to support it upright. One of them would have had to stay with the bike, sitting astride it, feet in the mud to keep it upright. But . . . could Penny, with her shoes in the mud, have managed to support the bike? I think not. Her feet wouldn't have been large enough. But Philip would have had hefty riding boots, Penny something more delicate. It was obvious who had to stay with the bike—Philip. They could've gone away, and come back another time. But you know how it is—if you've worked yourself into the proper pitch of determination . . . well, it has to be carried through. The home of Sylvia Thomas was perhaps a hundred yards away. Maybe a little further. So . . . I expect they decided what to do from their respective footwear at that time. Only Philip could stay with the bike. I'm sure they would have realised it.'

'You're making this up!' shouted Penny. 'There's not a word of truth in it.'

But to the team of firefighters around us, my reconstruction, though it in no way included Charlie's death, was acceptable. They felt that they only had to wait, and that I would shortly be working my way round to what really interested them, and they stood there, stiff and silent.

'You'll know, Penny,' I said, 'how much of it I'm making up to fit the background facts. I can't *prove* that you and Philip were there that night.'

'We weren't. Weren't!' she shouted up into my face.

'But Philip's already told me,' I said to her patiently, 'that *he* was there. Followed his mother, he said. But he didn't tell me whether he had taken you along with him, that evening. Did he do that, Penny?'

She shook her head violently, her shock of hair not flying around, as it normally would. She had no cover for it. It was sodden, a jumbled mass of saturated hair.

'I think,' I said, 'that when I ask him—which it seems I'll have to do, round at Mr Fisher's office—he'll probably agree that you were with him that evening, the night Sylvia died—and he'll no doubt, with the best of intentions, tell us that it was he who supported his own motor bike, in all that mud, because you couldn't have done so, and that you, Penny, and not Philip, were the one who went to Sylvia's house, to warn her away from Philip's father. All right, all right . . .'

I caught her flying fist in mid-air, caught it by the wrist, and shook it a little before thrusting it back at her. 'It's lies . . . all lies!' Penny shouted.

'I believe not,' I said. 'Philip can hardly claim that it was you who stayed with the bike. You could not have supported it, Penny. You're simply not physically large enough,

219

especially in all that mud. So Philip had to sit astride it, while you went to pay a visit to his father's mistress, and I'd expect that you didn't intend the whole visit to flare up into fury and violence. And Sylvia died.'

'It's all lies!' she shouted, repeating herself. 'Lies!'

'If only I could prove that!' I said. 'But I can't. It's not, Penny, and you know it. I don't know whose temper flared up first—but I do know that your hand was the one that fell on the rolling-pin.'

'You can't say that!'

'Oh yes, I can. And I'm sure that Philip will claim that it was he who killed her. Very noble, Philip can be. But . . . I think . . . a little less noble than he was . . . because certain other things have to be considered.'

'Is he mad?' Penny demanded, looking round at our tight group of police and firefighters. I could feel what they were thinking, if only because not a single voice had intruded into what I'd been saying.

Penny's confidence, I could feel, was crumbling away. She knew that we had not yet considered the death of Harry—and the death of Charlie.

'You're not to say that!' Penny screamed.

I wasn't sure what I should now say, in her reckoning. I had to reconstruct her actions and movements, to understand what they must have been.

'Philip must have known,' I explained to her. 'When I arrested Connie for the killing of Sylvia Thomas, Philip said nothing. There! Everything isn't black and revolting. Philip's stood by you, even though it meant his mother had to go to prison. All the way through.'

'What's he saying?' she screamed, flinging her arms around, nearly dislodging her shoulder bag from her shoulder. She was very close to hysteria.

'I'm saying,' I told her, 'that I can support everything I've said. I'm saying that Philip might not go on covering for you, when he realises that it was you who killed his father. You knew the Land Rover was there, in the vicinity of the murder of Sylvia Thomas, and that Harry must have known that it was you who killed Sylvia Thomas. But Harry kept quiet about what he knew. It wasn't just to oblige you. He was protecting his son, your Philip. Because he thought that Philip could be charged as an accessory. So he kept quiet, and I arrested Philip's mother. There . . . you see. He must have thought very highly of you. You'll no doubt consider that to be flattering. To be admired—as a murderess! What flattery!'

I couldn't go on. My voice was failing. I longed to light my pipe—and Amelia was in tears, a handkerchief clasped to her face.

And around me, the firefighters were silent, unmoving.

'But it ran away with you, Penny, didn't it?' I asked her. She was unable to speak, was stiff with fear, as the firefighters were mumbling amongst each other, like distant thunder. Threatening thunder.

'It's all lies!' Penny whispered. 'All lies!' She seemed to be short of breath.

'But no,' I said. 'Because it all follows logically. Harry could have known the truth. He was there, at the site of Sylvia's death. So . . . Harry was a threat. He had to die. It was as straightforward as that. And unfortunately, you thought Charlie witnessed *that* killing.'

Now, at last, the firefighters were hearing what they had wished for. The truth of the death of Charlie.

'Harry knew, or guessed, the truth,' I went on. 'You *must* have realised that. He kept quiet about it while Connie was in prison, but when she came out she asked me to reopen the investigation. You'd feel the threat. You had to make a move. A phone call. "Meet me at ten, by the paddling pool." *This* paddling pool, Penny. So he came here, and you were waiting, with a weapon. A blow to the crown of his head. Oh . . . . you must have perfected it by that time.'

'It's all lies!' she burst out. Too long, she had kept silent, her mind scrambling around for a way out. Any way out.

'Not lies,' I said.

And around us there was a silence, more

frightening than a roar of fury could have been. Yet, fury was there, etched in every face. They stood there, motionless—ten men, who still clung to their hoses, silent, absorbing it all. Then, a whisper from one of them. 'Bitch!' Penny whirled around, a response on her lips I was certain.

But she did not make it. One solitary hosepipe operator reacted. With his equipment still adjusted to 'fine spray', he gave it the last flick it needed, and the spray hit her face. 'Bitch!' he said, but this time it was not a whisper.

Penny took a step back, half raising a palm; beseeching, I thought. It might have been a signal, as they all reacted. All ten hoses were operated. Spray masked her, head to feet. I got the edge of it. She took another step back, but this time there was only an inch or two of the pool's rim behind her foot, and the rims were rounded. She staggered. Three more hoses, now on their main setting of direct power, completed the move. She slipped, and toppled over backwards into a foot of water, rolled over, staggered to her feet, and all ten jets of water caught her, flung her back, rolled her over again. She tried to rise, but every hose now assaulted her. She staggered, her arm around her head and her face down. The shoulder bag obstructed her movements. As she lifted her head, the jets thrust her back, and her head went under.

'You damned idiots!' I shouted. 'You'll drown her.'

It had no effect. I watched as her head came up. She was clearly close to exhaustion, mouth wide open, gasping for air. She was on her knees now, on concrete. They pummelled her with water.

'You damned fools!' I shouted. 'She's drowning.'

But again, my appeal had no effect. There was only one move I could make. I thrust Sheba's lead into Amelia's hand. Jake was already beside her, panting.

'No, Richard!' she screamed.

I jumped in. The dogs tried to get to me, and Amelia had to release them, or be pulled after me. Penny was being hampered by her shoulder bag. Gasping, I tried to get it from her. 'No!' she tried to shout. I read the word on her lips and in her expression. The dogs got their teeth into it, and pulled.

Now she had to release it. There was no other possible action she could take. Happy now, the dogs brought it to me. But I had Penny to consider. I took the shoulder bag from them and threw it as far as I could towards the edge of the pool. I'm a very poor thrower, but this time I got it right, and it fell with a clatter at Amelia's feet. At once, the dogs ran to retrieve it, and brought it back to me. Just what I didn't want. I lifted Penny from her crouch in the water, but she collapsed against me. All I could do, hampered by the assistance offered by Sheba and Jake, was to hook my hands beneath Penny's arms, and drag her to the side. Now the dogs followed me, bringing the shoulder bag with them. Dimly, because the noise and the water had deafened me, I heard Amelia shout to the dogs. They went to her, taking the shoulder bag between them.

The group, who had nearly drowned Penny, now stood in silence, their limp hoses flopping around their feet, dribbling water into the pool. Abruptly, the anger and hatred had run from me. The dogs jumped up on to the pavement slabs and stared down, heads cocked at me, as I crawled over the rim of the pool. Several hands reached down to help me to my feet. They were all silent, aware that their behaviour had been shameful. Penny staggered a few feet away, to the grass surface, where she could sit, cover her face with her hands, and weep.

I was no longer aware of what was going on around me, and the dogs thrust themselves to my side, whining.

Then, abruptly, Fisher was standing in front of me, staring down with an expression of extreme disfavour.

'Can't you keep out of trouble, Patton?' he asked wearily.

'I try. I assure you, Super, that I try.'

'I've got an ambulance coming,' he said.

'Ambulance!' I glanced at Amelia, who was pouting her displeasure.

'Not for you,' he said. 'For this young lady.' He gestured towards Penny, who was at once alert, twisting her head around, her eyes searching for Philip.

'I shall be sending a WPC with her,' Fisher went on. 'To sit beside her bed, until she's fit to travel.'

'Travel?' I asked, wondering why Philip was not with us.

'Travel,' said Fisher. 'But not far. To my office. Where I intend to charge her with a number of crimes.'

'Such as murders?' I asked.

'I have that in mind.'

I was groping for my pipe, trusting that my tobacco pouch would have kept its contents usable.

'Then,' I suggested, 'if it's murder you're pursuing, I suggest that you up-end that shoulder bag of hers . . .'

But he was already making a move towards it. Penny made protesting sounds, but Fisher did as I suggested. What clattered on to the paving slabs included a hefty adjustable spanner, the same one as I had seen Penny wielding, the first time I'd met her.

'And there's your weapon, Super,' I said. 'Now—may we go home?'

I glanced at Amelia, including her in that request. She nodded eagerly. 'Home,' she said longingly. 'You've got spare slacks in the car, and your anorak.'

So we went with Fisher to the sub-police office, Amelia impatient. They fixed us up with the necessary facilities required to dry me out, they produced a quantity of brandy to set my blood racing, and, Amelia having filled in the waiting time by towelling the dogs dry, we all said polite goodbyes, and Fisher said he would be in touch.

I slept during the whole of the trip home, on the rear seat between Sheba and Jake. No chance of catching a chill, when you're smothered with warm dogs.